"You're afraid of me, aren't you?"
Mary asked.

"That's the dumbest thing you've ever said...
and I've heard you say some pretty dumb things,"
Hank replied.

Sliding behind the steering wheel, Mary donned her
duster, hat and glasses. "You are. Of course, you're
not going to admit it, but you are. It's so ridiculous.
I'm not in the least afraid of you, and maybe I should
be. Why men like women who blush and pout and
say anything but what's really on their minds is
beyond me."

Hank studied her a second, his eyes dark and
confused. "What I feel toward you, Mary, is so...
so damned complicated that I...I don't even know
how to describe it. Mary, you just don't understand."

"That's what I'm fond of accusing you of—not
understanding—and I don't think you do half the
time. But I do understand you, Hank. Truly I do. So
much more than you could ever imagine."

Barbara Kaye is acknowledged as the author of this work.

Special thanks and acknowledgment to Sutton Press Inc. for its contribution to the concept for the Crystal Creek series.

ISBN 0-373-82530-7

LET'S TURN BACK THE YEARS

Barbara Kaye

LET'S TURN BACK THE YEARS

Harlequin Books

TORONTO • NEW YORK • LONDON
AMSTERDAM • PARIS • SYDNEY • HAMBURG
STOCKHOLM • ATHENS • TOKYO • MILAN
MADRID • WARSAW • BUDAPEST • AUCKLAND

Dear Reader,

Here's what the reviewers had to say about our twelfth Crystal Creek installment, Barbara Kaye's *Everybody's Talkin'*:

"Ms. Kaye masterfully blends the old and the new and adds just the right touch of mystery to make this a thoroughly enjoyable trip to Crystal Creek."

—*Romantic Times*

This month, the talented Ms. Kaye, who first introduced you to Crystal Creek with *Deep in the Heart,* and followed it with *After the Lights Go Out* and *Everybody's Talkin',* weaves the tale Crystal Creek fans have long been waiting for, the decades-long story of the irrepressible, cranky, clairvoyant Hank Travis—from his humble origins as a peanut farmer's son, to his astonishing rise to fortune in the booming Texas oil fields!

Margot Dalton returns next month, and she'll take us back to the Double Bar for another visit with Brock and Amanda, and, of course, Alvin. While Brock and Amanda contend with the strain on their relationship imposed by Brock's aunt Millie, Alvin manages to befriend an exploring young couple and land in a hole he can barely survive!

Watch for *Never Givin' Up on Love,* available wherever Harlequin books are sold. And stick around in Crystal Creek—home of sultry Texas drawls, smooth Texas charm and tall, sexy Texans!

Marsha Zinberg
Coordinator, Crystal Creek

A Note from the Author

The forty years between the oil gusher at Spindletop and America's entry into World War II were but a blink of the eye in history's span, but they gave rise to a legend that remains alive in popular imagination.

The Texas oilman—a coarse, hard-drinking, up-from-nothing type who was more of a gambler than anything. He obtained leases by whatever means, drilled wildcats, fought "interference" from anyone, and, so the legend persists, ended up with more money than he could spend. Hank Travis was, more or less, such a man.

But no one begins life that way. This is the story of the young Hank Travis, and I hope that readers who have taken the citizens of Crystal Creek to heart will enjoy it.

Barbara Kaye

Who's Who in Crystal Creek

Have you missed the story of one of your favorite Crystal Creek characters? Here's a quick guide to help you easily locate the titles and story lines:

Available at your local bookseller, or see the Crystal Creek back-page ad for reorder information.

PROLOGUE

Hank Travis was described in many ways during his lifetime, and though the descriptions varied and were often contradictory, to some extent they all were accurate.

He was single-minded even as a boy, always certain of what he wanted, and none of his dreams had a thing to do with a South Texas farm. Later in life, when I knew him, he was orncry, cantankerous, profane, strong-willed and opinionated. He never wasted a minute saying something he didn't mean, nor did he hesitate to say exactly what was on his mind, no matter whose toes got stepped on or whose ears burned.

But there was no meanness in him, and he was as fiercely loyal as he was independent. It was said that if you had him for a friend, you didn't need too many others.

J. T. McKINNEY RAISED his head and let his pen come to rest on the paper. Rubbing his eyes, he stared at the wall of his study. He still found it so hard to believe Hank was gone, particularly since there had been no illness, nothing one could give as the immediate cause of death. There had simply been a gradual decline, and to J.T. it seemed to have begun right after Jeff Harris's death. Hank had been vicariously reliving his own youth through the young oiler, and Jeff's death in a rig accident had been a terrible blow to the old man.

J.T. looked down at the paper on his desk. He wondered if he was up to this....

When the editor of the Crystal Creek paper had approached him four days after his grandfather's funeral, wanting to do a feature article on Hank Travis for some future Sunday edition, it had sounded simple. Just jot down something about his grandfather's life, human interest stuff.

But it wasn't simple, J.T. now realized, because Hank had not led a simple life. There was so much to be said that he was at a loss as to where to begin. But then, Hank would have said the beginning was always a good place. Sighing, J.T. picked up his pen and resumed writing.

He was born on December 12, 1893, and for the first eighteen years of his life he lived with his parents and siblings on a peanut farm in South Texas. But from the age of eight he knew he wasn't going to be a farmer. That was the year the Spindletop gusher blew in. Newspaper accounts of the momentous event thrilled young Hank, and he somehow knew the oil fields were where adventure lay. When he was eighteen, he struck out for Oklahoma and his own personal pot of gold at the end of the rainbow.

Men like Hank were largely responsible for creating the legend of the fiercely independent Texas oilman. The search for black gold attracted a certain type of individual—one with sass and vinegar in his veins and a gambler's instincts in his heart. Hank's story is the story of the twentieth century, the development of an industry and a state.

And ultimately it is the story of a woman. Hank knew many women during his extremely long life, but he truly loved only one. Her name was Mary, and if my grandfather were here today, he would insist that this be Mary's story, too, for like Hank, she epitomized her era.

CHAPTER ONE

Spring—1912

THE NARROW, DUSTY ROAD rose ahead for seemingly endless miles. A lone young man trudged along it. Pausing occasionally, he squinted his eyes in the dust-laden air and looked behind him, hoping to see a farm wagon heading for town. His footsore journey was half an hour old, and he hadn't seen a thing to indicate anyone lived anywhere near this lonely road. He wasn't even sure where he was—somewhere southwest of Fort Worth was his guess, his hope. If he could just get to Fort Worth, he'd buy a ticket on the Santa Fe and be in Oklahoma in no time. He'd been planning it so long. Half of his life, it seemed.

He continued walking north. In one hand he carried a battered valise that contained everything he owned in the world. He thrust the other hand into his trousers pocket and fingered the money there. Ten dollars and some change. He'd never get to Guthrie, Oklahoma on ten dollars, so he was going to have to stop somewhere and work for a few months. That kind of delay annoyed him, but there was nothing else he could do.

He had been hitching rides for three days, walking when he had to, sleeping wherever he could. Last night it had been in a friendly farmer's barn. Now his stomach was complaining noisily. He'd made do with the coffee and doughnut the farmer had given him for breakfast, and tried not to think about how much hungrier he might get if he didn't find work soon.

Pausing again, he set the valise on the ground and ran his fingers through the thick thatch of dark hair atop his head. He was thin, of medium height, and had dark, brooding eyes. He looked older than his actual age, which was eighteen, and nothing about his frail, shabby appearance gave evidence of the resolve that drove him. Belief in himself was all he owned—that and ten dollars, a few old clothes and a fierce determination never to plow ground again. The South Texas farm he had left three days ago meant nothing to him. He had fulfilled the one solemn promise he had made to his father: he had stayed in school until he graduated. Now he was on his way to Oklahoma and the oil fields, to the Promised Land.

To think that only a few months ago he had been willing to give up his dream of Oklahoma, all because of Billie Jean Surratt. Blonde, blue-eyed and beautiful, the doctor's daughter had allowed him to kiss and fondle her until he forgot all about anything else. His dreams had gone soaring off into the sky, and he'd fallen hopelessly in love. When he finally managed to stammer as much to her, vowing to work as hard as he could to give her everything she deserved, Billie Jean had eyed him curiously.

"But, honey, I thought we were just having fun. Shoot, I didn't think you'd take any of our foolin' around *seriously*. I can't make any plans for years and years. You see, I have to go to college first. Then there will be a year in Europe. Mama and Daddy have it all planned. In fact, they want me to stop seeing so much of you since... well, since nothing's ever going to come of it."

The rejection had humiliated him. He'd been so bitterly heartbroken that he'd wrapped himself in a cocoon of misery for days, but now he had emerged with only a lingering bad memory and a hard lesson learned. A poor peanut farmer's boy could never have a doctor's daughter, not in a million years. He hoped he never forgot that.

So he had embraced the dream of Oklahoma with renewed fervor. Saying goodbye to his parents had been harder than he'd expected it to be. After all, he'd been talking about Oklahoma a long time. His mother had shed a few tears, and his father had looked as though he wanted to. His older brothers had stood by awkwardly, gaping at him with a mixture of disbelief and envy. The baby of the family had followed him all the way to the front gate, extracting a promise that his brother would send him something from Oklahoma. And the young man planned to send them all something when he drew his first big pay. Everyone said a fellow could make a lot of money in the oil fields.

His thoughts were interrupted by the sound of horses' hooves and the rattling of wheels. Turning quickly, he saw a fine-looking rig bearing down on him. Waving frantically, he sighed with relief when the buggy slowed and came to a halt. A rugged, weathered face under a spotless wide-brimmed hat peered at him.

"Need a lift into town, son?" the man asked.

"Yes, sir!" Grabbing the valise, the young man climbed aboard, relieved to hear there *was* a town nearby.

The man stuck out his hand. "Name's Duncan MacGregor, son."

"Hank Travis, Mr. MacGregor. Sure appreciate the ride."

MacGregor flicked the reins, and the wagon moved forward. "Going somewhere in particular?"

"Not really. Just to the nearest place I can find some temporary work. I need to make enough money to get me on up to Oklahoma."

"Got family in Oklahoma?"

"No."

They bounced along the bumpy road a few minutes before MacGregor asked, "Running away from home, son?"

"Oh, no, sir. I just sorta...left. Been thinking about it a long time. Won't be nobody comin' to look for me, if that's what you mean."

"So why Oklahoma?"

"The oil fields," Hank said. "The Cushing Field. Maybe you've heard of it."

MacGregor scowled. "Don't pay much attention to the oil business. There's some folks doing a little prospecting close to my place, but I figure it's just a passing fancy. They'll all be gone soon, and I can't say it won't be good riddance." He shifted to look at Hank. "So you need to find some work, huh? Tell you what, Hank. Up this road a few miles is a town called Slaterton, and about ten miles past is my place, the YH Ranch. Fourteen thousand acres of paradise and some of the finest Herefords in the country. We always need hands. Twenty-five dollars a month and all the tobacco you want. A good bed and plenty of good food. Nobody feeds better'n we do."

Hank did some rapid mental calculation. Twenty-five a month was more money than he'd ever made, but he knew he could make almost that much a week in the oil fields. But he wasn't in the oil fields, not yet. With room and meals thrown in, he would hardly have to spend any of that money.

He could be on his way to Oklahoma in two months, three at the most.

Of course, ranching wasn't exactly what he'd had in mind when he thought of finding work. Ranching was too much like farming to suit him. But he was hardly in a position to be particular.

"Thanks, Mr. MacGregor. That's mighty nice of you. I'll do my best to make you a good hand."

"You might find you like it, son. Beats hell out of that filthy oil field work."

"Can I ask you something?"

"Ask away."

"Why is your place called the YH Ranch?"

MacGregor smiled. "You'll see," he said, and within minutes he drove the buggy into the shabby outskirts of unscenic Slaterton, Texas.

At first glance it didn't look like much of a town. Hank spotted a general store and another that catered to women. There was a bank, a barbershop, a livery and a tiny post office, plus a boardinghouse that advertised home cooking. He also spotted a café named after someone called Barney. The Texas and Pacific Railroad tracks ran along the southern edge of the town, and there was a ramshackle depot beside them. That was encouraging. When the time came, he wouldn't have to go far to catch a train.

Then they rode on a little farther, and suddenly the scene changed dramatically. On either side of the dirt thoroughfare, a dozen or more saloons and roadhouses stood, and even in the middle of the day they seemed to be doing a booming business. Everything appeared to have been erected hastily of raw lumber, with no thought to permanence. Beyond the saloons was what looked like an entire city of tents.

"Didn't figure a town way out here would be so busy," Hank commented, looking at the astonishing array of wagons, buggies and horses milling about the street.

MacGregor uttered a sound of derision. "Son, five years ago this was the nicest little town in the world. But I wouldn't give you a plugged nickel for the whole damn place now. This is what oilers do to a town—bring in guns and gamblers and whores ... just a mess of trouble."

Hank tried unsuccessfully to envision Slaterton as the nicest little town in the world. Down in South Texas he'd heard it said of a particularly worthless piece of property that at least it helped hold the rest of the world together, and he guessed that was the best he would say about this depressing little community.

MacGregor drove through town, acknowledging the waves of half a dozen people, and soon Slaterton was behind them. Then suddenly, out in the middle of nowhere, they passed another building, little more than a tin shack that was surrounded by a barbed-wire fence. Huge stacks of pipe filled the yard. Over the door of the building was a sign that read Holt Petroleum Company.

MacGregor jerked his head in that direction. "Those are the fellows who've been pestering me about drilling an oil well on my land."

"You don't want a well, Mr. MacGregor?" Hank asked in some surprise.

"No! I don't want the noise spooking my herd, and I don't want a bunch of wagons trampling my grass. Besides, there's no oil down there."

"How do you know that?"

"I've been digging for water for twenty-five years. If there was any oil down there, I'd have found it myself."

Hank shifted in the seat and studied the rancher with interest. It took him only a few seconds to decide that if MacGregor wasn't the image of the perfect Texas cowboy, he came close enough to it. He was somewhere around fifty, Hank guessed, and looked as tough and strong as a bull. His face was weathered, his features chiseled and completely masculine. The dark hair beneath his hat was thick, and it curled around his shirt collar. He had heavy brows and blue eyes that disappeared into slits in his face when he smiled or scowled. It was easy to imagine him sitting ramrod straight in a saddle. He was so different from Hank's father, who was bent and stooped from a lifetime at a plow.

Abruptly, MacGregor guided the team and wagon off the main road and drove under an iron arch that proclaimed the entrance to the YH Ranch. Ahead, perhaps a mile from the arch, stood the most impressive house Hank had ever seen. It was two-storied and built of brick that had been painted the color of daffodils. An iron-pillared veranda ran all around the bottom story.

"YH Ranch," Hank murmured, looking at the rancher. "Yellow House, right?"

"Right. Isn't she the prettiest sight you ever saw?"

"I reckon she is. No one back home, not even the big landowners, have anything that grand."

MacGregor pulled the team to a halt at the side of the house. Immediately, it seemed out of no-where, a cowboy appeared to unhitch the horses. He looked to be in his twenties and wore standard cowboy garb. "Get your visitin' done, Duncan?"

"That I did. Tend to the horses, Jed, and then get this fellow settled in. His name's Hank Travis, and he's going to be working for us."

The man named Jed cast a doubtful look in Hank's direction and told him, "Wait here. I'll be right back."

"I'll see you later, son," MacGregor said, giving Hank a hearty slap on the back before turning to go into the house.

Hank stood in the middle of the side yard, feeling alone and out of place, and waited for Jed to return. He studied his surroundings. From the looks of things, MacGregor was doing all right in the cattle business. His ranch, a cluster of yellow buildings smack in the middle of wide-open prairie, looked prosperous.

Hank slowly pivoted as he tried to take in everything at once. Suddenly his gaze fell on a lone figure standing on the back veranda, staring off into the distance. It was a girl, a little younger than he was, he guessed. Her long dark hair was tied at the nape with a big bow. She wore a print dress that came to her ankles and was sashed at her tiny waist. Its puff sleeves billowed, then fit closely at her wrists. Her profile was enchanting—long, slender neck and upturned nose.

Then she turned, and Hank found himself staring at a face an artist would have been hard-pressed to improve on. He was sure he had never seen anyone so pretty. She was prettier even than Billie Jean. For a fleeting second their eyes locked. Hers were big and round and dark, and instead of dipping demurely, they looked at him fully, almost boldly. It was an unexpected reaction, to say the least. Most girls were so shy... or pretended to be.

"Hello," he managed to say.

"Hello," the girl replied. She stared at him openly for a second or two, a hint of a smile playing at the corners of her mouth. She seemed about to say something, but at that moment a voice sounded from inside the house. The enchanting girl turned and fled, as though she'd seen a snake.

Hank stared after her, and was still staring when the cowboy named Jed returned. "Okay, Travis, come with me and I'll show you your bunk."

Hank fell into step beside him, and Jed led him to a long yellow building near the corral. "Where was the last place you worked?" Jed asked, as he pushed open the door to the bunkhouse.

"This is my first job...unless you want to count working on my family's farm."

Jed made some kind of sound deep in his throat. "A real greenhorn, huh? How old are you?"

"Eighteen."

Another funny sound. Jed's boot heels clomped along the wooden floor of the deserted bunkhouse. "This'll be your bunk, and that's your locker. My room's down there." He indicated a closed door at the far end of the big room. "Dining room's on the right. There's a bathhouse out back. Hot water every Saturday night. You want to bathe more'n that, you do it in cold water."

Hank dropped his valise on the bunk. "How come you rate a room of your own?"

"I'm kinda the assistant foreman of this operation. Foreman's name is Matt Slocum, but you won't be having much truck with him. Duncan gives him orders, Matt gives 'em to me, and I give 'em to the men. Matt's got his own house out back a ways." Jed looked Hank up and down. "You're gonna have to get you some real working clothes—boots and some of Mr. Levi Strauss's britches. A hat, too."

"I don't have money for clothes," Hank protested.

"Duncan'll buy. He hired you, so he'll outfit you."

"He seems like a pretty nice man."

"The best." Jed stuck out his hand. "Jed Purcell, Hank. Welcome to the YH."

Hank took the hand and shook it the way his father had told him men shook hands—hard and firm. "Say, Jed, who was the girl I saw standing on the porch a minute ago?"

"Girl? Must've been Mary Margaret, Duncan's niece. Long dark hair?"

"That's the one."

"Don't get too close."

"Why? She got something catchin'?"

Jed grinned. "No, but Duncan don't let her anywhere near the cowhands. The only person around here who's allowed to talk to her is Matt."

"How old is she?"

Jed shrugged. "Sixteen, I think. I probably haven't said three words to her since I got here. I'm not allowed to talk to her, either."

"Mr. MacGregor's niece, huh? Does he have any kids of his own?"

Jed shook his head. "Nope. And his wife died ten years ago, so he's all alone. Maybe that's why he's so protective of Mary Margaret. She's his youngest brother's kid. The brother died of pneumonia a few years back, and Duncan persuaded her mama to let Mary Margaret live with him so she could go to some fancy ladies' academy in Fort Worth. She's not around here much—too busy learning to be a lady and all. This is spring vacation, or she wouldn't be here now."

"Snooty?" Hank asked.

"Sorta. That's what they teach girls in those places. Just remember to give her a wide berth."

"Don't worry," Hank said with an edge to his voice. "I've had some experience with that kind."

Jed reached out and slapped him on the shoulder. "Come on, I'll show you around."

"What am I gonna be doing around here?"

Jed grinned again, wider this time. "Everything nobody else wants to do. That's what greenhorns are for."

FROM HER BEDROOM WINDOW on the second floor of the big yellow house, Mary watched Jed and the new hand leave the bunkhouse. Sighing, she sat on the edge of her bed. The newcomer was kind of cute-looking, but she'd bet he was just like all the rest of them—half-literate and wild as the devil. Cowhands all seemed to be cut of the same cloth.

Not that it mattered if the new man was as handsome as Adonis and a veritable genius, with the soul of a saint. Duncan wouldn't let her have anything to do with him. Sometimes she thought it would be nice to talk to a boy somewhere near her own age, but she guessed that would have to wait until she was out of school and on her own. At Mayberry Academy, males of any kind were as scarce as vine-ripe tomatoes at Christmas.

Her eyes idly roamed the familiar surroundings. It was a nice room, so much nicer than the one she'd had on the farm outside Crystal Creek. Her uncle lived elegantly. He had a cook, plus a mother-and-daughter team who cleaned his house and clucked over Mary like a couple of mother hens. She didn't have to lift so much as a finger. That, she knew, was the way proper ladies lived. It was a far cry from Crystal Creek.

She rose and went to the cheval glass to inspect her appearance. In an hour or so, she would be expected to join her uncle in his study. Maybe Matt Slocum would be there, maybe not. If he was, she would drink fruit punch while he and her uncle partook of sippin' whiskey, and she would listen to them expound on whatever subject had currently grabbed their interest. Usually it was the weather or the market or, occasionally, "the mess" in Washington, D.C.

Then the three of them would go to dinner, and afterward the men would smoke, drink brandy and play cards. The routine varied only when Duncan had guests, and that didn't happen nearly often enough to suit Mary. Neither her uncle nor Matt ever asked her opinion about anything, no doubt feeling she had no opinions... or wasn't supposed to, if she did. How shocked they would have been to learn of the things that spun around in her head. Sometimes she thought her brain would burst.

Two more days of her vacation were left; then it was back to the restrictiveness of the academy. But that was infinitely better than having stayed in Crystal Creek and ended up married to a farm boy and having five or six babies. At the academy she was learning something—not just the social graces, but how to type and do bookkeeping. She hoped her mother and brothers did not expect her to return to the farm after she graduated. And she so hoped her uncle did not think her future lay at YH Ranch. If they did, they were all destined to be greatly disappointed. There was such a big world out there, and so many things were happening in it. The object of an education at Mayberry Academy was most definitely not to teach young ladies what they had missed all their lives, but that was precisely the effect it had had on Mary.

In a year she would graduate. Three months after that she would turn eighteen. Her plans were to get a job in a business organization, perhaps a bank, and find a room to rent. There was a respectable hotel in Fort Worth, she'd heard—one that catered strictly to proper single ladies. She got so excited just thinking about it.

One year and three months. Forever!

HANK DID NOT EVEN CATCH another glimpse of Mary before she returned to the academy. He was too busy. He had thought farming was the last word in hard work, but it was nothing compared to this slave labor. For one thing, though he'd been riding horses since he was knee-high to a grasshopper, he wasn't used to spending long, long hours in the saddle. He wondered if the aches and pains would ever subside.

For another, Jed had been correct when he'd said Hank would get all the jobs no one else wanted. His first full day on the job was spent riding from one end of the ranch to the other, gathering cow chips— "prairie coal", they were called. The chuck cook used them for his stove. With all the cows on the ranch, the chips weren't hard to find, but gathering dried cow dung was not high on Hank's list of desirable employments.

The second day, he plowed fireguards. Standing behind that plow brought back so many unpleasant memories, he almost quit on the spot. The third day was better; he actually got to work with the herd. He wasn't much good at it, but he watched the others and learned. "There's nothing so-so about being a cowboy, Hank," Jed had told him. "You either love it or hate it. If you love it, you wouldn't do anything else. If you hate it, you'd do *anything* else." Hank couldn't say he had fallen in love with it, not by any means, but by the end of the first week, he decided he just might make it for a couple of months.

And the day finally came when he no longer was thought of as the greenest of greenhorns. He knew he had been accepted when a Saturday payday rolled around and he was invited to join the rest of the men for a sojourn into Slaterton that night.

"What do you do there?" Hank asked Jed.

"Go to Gracie's or one of the other places. Drink some whiskey, maybe get a woman."

"Women go to places where there's whiskey?"

"A certain kind do."

It sounded wicked... and utterly fascinating. Hank momentarily thought of the money in his pocket. His total worth was now thirty-five dollars and some change. He hadn't spent a cent since coming to the YH, and he needed every dime to get to Oklahoma. But in the end, he found himself piling into the ranch wagon with half a dozen other hands for the ride into town.

Slaterton went wild on Saturday night. It was experiencing a boom that had attracted an odd assortment of characters—people who had left played-out oil fields, people who had walked away from poor farms to look for better luck elsewhere, along with the inevitable gamblers, quack medicine men and prostitutes who followed the booms. When reinforced by cowboys in from ranches and roughnecks in from well sites, they made for a boisterous crowd.

Gracie's was located in the middle of the two-block-long strip of dance halls and roadhouses. Though it was early, the joint was already crowded with customers. Hank and Jed took a booth in the rear under a sign that proclaimed there was a fifty-dollar fine for fighting, a house rule that Hank imagined was totally unenforceable. There was another that read: If you believe in credit, loan me $5.

They had just sat down when a pudgy waitress with rouged cheeks appeared to take their order. Within minutes she had returned with two glasses of whiskey. Hank hesitantly took a sip, then grimaced and coughed. "Good God, Jed! This stuff is terrible!"

"It is, isn't it? God only knows what's in it." Jed took a long drink, then set down his glass, wiped his mouth on his shirtsleeve and studied his companion. "I gotta hand it to you, Hank. First time I saw you I'd have sworn you wouldn't last three days."

Hank stiffened in automatic reflex to what he considered a reference to his lack of brawn. Then he relaxed. Jed was a good man without a trace of malice in him. "I've worked a time or two in my day."

"Apparently."

The two men sat in silence a minute, nursing their drinks. Hank wasn't accustomed to drinking whiskey, but on this night, in this place, the stuff was almost refreshing. He felt good about himself, proud of having survived those difficult first days, pleased to have been accepted by Jed and the others. It was good to be away from raising peanuts, good to be making money on his own, good to be just that much closer to Oklahoma.

"Do you know where you are, Hank?" Jed suddenly asked. "The armpit of civilization, that's where. A few years back you couldn't *give* this real estate to anyone but a few old ranchers who liked living away from everything."

"Then why are you here?"

"This is where the money ran out. I was on my way to California at the time. I got hired on at the YH, and I found out I like bein' a cowpoke. Don't reckon I'll ever make California, and I sure as hell don't want to go back to Arkansas." Jed motioned to the waitress to bring them another round. "But

I don't figure you for staying. Where're you headed?''

"Oklahoma."

"Why Oklahoma?"

"The oil fields . . . where the money is."

Jed chuckled. "Not for folks like you and me, Hank. The ones who bring oil out'a the ground aren't the ones who make money. It's the guys who own it once it's up."

"I know that, Jed," Hank said. "Just like the only guys who make money off'a ranching are the ones who own lots of land. Owning oil is what I'm talking about."

The waitress put fresh drinks down on the table and carried away the empty glasses. Jed was studying Hank thoughtfully. Finally he said, "Well, maybe so. I'd be the last to tell a fellow he can't do something he's set his mind to." Jed took a hefty swallow of whiskey and stood. "'Scuse me a minute, Hank. I just saw someone I need to talk to. Be right back."

Hank watched Jed walk away, then settled down to survey the scenery. Gracie's was full of the motleyest collection of human beings he had ever seen. He imagined that none of the women present had been to church recently. Some of the men looked like the kind he wouldn't want to encounter in a dark alley. More than a few of them were carrying firearms, something that apparently wasn't against the law in Slaterton. The noise level was atrocious. Across the room a piano player was banging away, seemingly oblivious to the deafening din. Hank noticed a steady stream of men and women going up and down the stairs that led to the second floor, so he had to assume that Gracie's was also a brothel, something he had only heard about.

He was grinning, enjoying watching everyone when a man approached his table. The man was about Jed's age but was no roughneck or cowboy, if looks were any indication. Tall and so slender he was almost skinny, he wore wire-rimmed eyeglasses, and his khakis were bandbox fresh. He looked something like a schoolteacher, thoroughly out of place in Gracie's.

"Excuse me," the man said. "I couldn't help overhearing your conversation with Jed Purcell, and I wondered if I could have a word with you. My name is Blue, James Blue. Jimmy to everyone. I'm a geologist with Holt Petroleum."

Hank couldn't imagine what the gentleman would want to talk to him about, but he said, "Sure. Have a seat. My name's Hank Travis."

Jimmy Blue slid into the seat Jed had just vacated. "Nice to meet you, Hank. You're interested in the oil business, I take it."

"Sure am. I'm working at the YH Ranch right now, but that's only temporary."

"How well do you know Duncan MacGregor?"

"I don't know him hardly at all. Why?"

"I need someone to introduce me to him, but I'm told he won't let oil people come anywhere near him."

"Why do you want to talk to him?"

"I got a proposition that anyone else would think irresistible. MacGregor won't even talk to me. I was hoping you might know him well enough to ask him to at least listen to me."

Hank shook his head. "I'm only a hired hand, Mr. Blue."

"Jimmy."

"Jimmy. I reckon Mr. MacGregor would be hard-pressed to remember my name." But Hank was curious about Jimmy Blue's proposition. "Do you mind telling me what it is you want him to hear?"

"Oh...about how I'd like to make him a millionaire."

"And he doesn't want that?" Hank asked in amazement.

"Apparently not. He said he was going to shoot the next oiler who showed up on his place." Jimmy grinned. "Takes all kinds, I suppose. But Elver sure wants that lease."

"Who's Elver?"

"Elver Holt, president of the company. He's an old hand at the oil business, if you figure fifteen years in it is old. His daddy was at Spindletop, and in oil circles, that's like having kinfolks at the Alamo. Elver's been all over Oklahoma. He knows the ropes."

"Then I guess you think there's oil on the YH, right?"

"An ocean of it . . . well, make that a sea. I'd bet on it. Of course, geology isn't an exact science by any means, and the general feeling's always been that you can drink every drop of oil in West Texas. But we've proven that wrong. Holt's drilled two producers, one on either side of MacGregor's place. Piddling wells, but that oil's coming from somewhere. I'm betting the mother lode is right under the YH Ranch."

Hank pondered this, fascinated and perplexed by Duncan MacGregor. To a poor farm kid from South Texas, it didn't make sense not to make as much money as a man could. "Wish I could help you, but if Mr. MacGregor won't listen to you folks, he's sure not gonna listen to me."

"Well, it was worth a try. Holt's going to get that lease sooner or later. Elver's persistent as hell." Jimmy paused and stared at Hank thoughtfully. "I heard you say you're on your way to Oklahoma."

"That's right...soon as I get some money saved."

"Better stick around here, kid. West Texas is where the action's going to be in a few years. You could be a pioneer." Jimmy stood, so Hank did, too. The two men shook hands. "Look me up and let me know how you're doing, Hank. And if I can be of service to you, just yell."

"Thanks, Jimmy. I'll do that."

Hank sat down and stared after the geologist's retreating figure. It was so odd. He was a nobody farm kid, and Jimmy Blue was an educated gentleman. Yet Hank experienced one of his intuitive feelings. He and Jimmy were going to be friends.

That night turned out to be a sort of rite of passage for him. He rolled his first cigarette and drank too much whiskey. He was introduced to Gracie herself, who said he was "cute," and later was propositioned by a prostitute who said the same thing. Had it not been for his lack of experience and his unwillingness to part with his hard-earned money, there was no telling what might have happened.

Then he and Jed ate a bowl of greasy stew at Barney's Café somewhere around eleven o'clock, just before piling into the wagon for the return trip to the YH. Hank felt so god-awful the next morning, he was sure he was coming down with some kind of sickness and was going to die at eighteen.

But that, the others assured him, was exactly the way a real cowboy was supposed to feel on Sunday morning.

CHAPTER TWO

AT SOME POINT in the distant past, Mary reflected as she stared out the window of her dormitory room, the people who built Mayberry Academy had gotten a real bargain on gray stone. The entire compound—the school, the dormitories, the teachers' residence, the tall wall that fenced it in—all were gray, gray, gray. Nothing—not the trees with their new leaves nor the May flowers—could do much to relieve the depressing dullness of the place. Surely Mayberry Academy had been designed by an aged monk.

It was Saturday afternoon, and the grounds were almost deserted, since many of the students lived close enough to go home on the weekend. Classes had ended at noon and would not resume until Monday morning. Mary felt rather sorry for the younger students, who were restricted to the school even on the weekend. At least she was an upperclassman and deemed sufficiently responsible to be trusted with an unchaperoned afternoon in town.

At that moment the door opened, and Harriet Warren, her roommate, flew into the room, out of breath as usual. Harriet hurried everywhere she went, forever appearing to have some important mission to take care of. "Mary, let's go to the moving pictures this afternoon."

"Oh, let's!"

"Do you have money? If not, I do," Harriet said.

"Yes. I've been very careful this month." It exasperated Mary that her uncle gave her such a tiny allowance—far, far less than Harriet's. Yet Duncan MacGregor couldn't imagine what a girl would want to spend money for. Didn't he pay the academy for her room and board and uniforms? Didn't the school furnish her with everything she needed for subsistence? What else besides a few personal toiletries could she possibly need to buy?

Mary had tried to explain that in a city like Fort Worth there were many shops full of things girls wanted, and that explanation had worked, after a fashion. Her uncle had recently increased her allowance, but only by a few dollars. So Mary was frugal, saving her money for important things like books, ice cream sodas... and, lately, the moving pictures.

"My uncle hates the cinematography shows," she said to Harriet, then giggled a little wickedly. "He says that watching pictures on a white curtain will corrupt young people and make them idle. That their brains will atrophy."

Harriet giggled, too, tossing her blond curls. "My father says they are innocent, merely the newest form of pantomime, and that they're here to stay. He says they'll only get more sophisticated as time goes by. He thinks that someday they'll be used to educate people."

Mary would never have been guilty of wishing she had, say, a different uncle or someone else for a mother, but she did so envy Harriet her parents. They were very modern. Her father was a newspaper editor, and her mother was a suffragette who had published several articles urging the vote for women. Mrs. Warren had even once lectured at Vassar. On the few weekends Mary had spent at their house, she had been astonished and fascinated at the talk around their dinner table. They discussed *ideas,* not the weather or the price of beef on the hoof, and they encouraged their daughter to do the same. The first time Chester Warren, Harriet's father, had asked Mary her opinion about something, she had been so startled she had been tongue-tied. Listening to the Warrens' conversations was far more of an education than she imagined she would ever receive at Mayberry Academy.

If Duncan MacGregor had any idea of the kind of young woman Harriet Warren was, he would have promptly asked the headmistress to find his

niece a more "suitable" roommate. Mary took
great pains never to voice the new ideas that were
beginning to fill her head, certainly not in front of
her uncle, and she was absolutely enchanted with
Harriet.

Harriet stood in front of a mirror, pinching her
cheeks to make them rosy. "You simply must read
the letter I received from Mama today," she said.
"It seems there was a big riot in front of the White
House last week. Fifteen thousand women were
picketing for the right to vote, and the police came
in and hit some of them and carried others off to
jail."

"How awful!" Mary cried.

Harriet turned from the mirror, eyes shining.
"Oh, no. It was exactly what the women wanted."

"To be beaten and taken to jail?"

"No, silly. Don't you see, Mary? They got a lot
of publicity and sympathy. The papers in the East
are full of articles about police brutality and injus-
tice, Mama says. She is absolutely delighted. Our
victory is inevitable. Daddy says so, too."

What a family! Mary recalled the one and only
time she had heard her uncle comment on wom-
en's suffrage. He'd said, "It's a man's privilege, his
duty to vote for his wife. Giving women the vote
would be shirking one's duty."

Fiddlesticks! Men like her uncle would never
change, but there were more and more men who

were beginning to stump for the cause. Changes were coming, and there was nothing anybody could do about it.

She and Harriet were so lucky to be living in such an enlightened age.

HANK HAD BEEN at the YH two months, and he felt wonderful. MacGregor had been right about the kind of food he would get. He'd never eaten so well or so often. He'd put on weight, which he'd needed, the exercise of his daily work had made him hard and tough. Ranching was a pretty healthy life, and he had to constantly caution himself against being seduced by it. In his letters to his parents—and he tried to be scrupulous about writing—he sounded as if he was having the time of his life. Maybe he was, but he would always remind himself that cowboys didn't get rich and oilers did. Every time he found himself in a state of self-satisfaction, he snapped out of it quickly.

At the end of May, Mary came back to the ranch for the summer. Hank saw her the day after her arrival. If anything, she was prettier than he remembered, and there were times when he would lie in his bunk at night and allow himself the luxury of wondering what it would be like to get close to her. But he was no fool; he knew he'd never find out. He'd been down *that* road before. Duncan would fire him in an instant if he even tried to, and he was beginning to amass riches, albeit twenty-five dollars at a time. Maybe someday, when he was in the oil business and had money in the bank, he could approach someone like Billie Jean Surratt or Mary Margaret MacGregor and not worry about being sent packing. In the meantime, he'd just keep working his fanny off and dreaming.

Actually, as it turned out, Mary was the first to approach him. It was a very warm afternoon in mid-June, and Hank was working a pair of horses in the main corral. Intent on the task at hand, he did not at first see the comely figure in the yellow frock watching him from outside the fence. When he did, he felt his heart leap up into his throat. Should he speak . . . or pretend he didn't see her?

He continued moving the horses in a circular pattern, and when he neared the spot where she stood, he slowed.

"Hello," she said.

Hank's tongue seemed to swell to twice its normal thickness. "Hello."

"My name's Mary."

"No, it isn't. It's Mary Margaret."

She gave him a peculiar look. "I like plain Mary best. Mary Margaret is such a mouthful."

"My name's Hank, Mary."

"How do you do."

He halted the horses in front of her, slapped their flanks and set them free to trot around the corral.

"I thought you weren't allowed to pass the time of day with the hired help."

She gave her head an impatient toss. "Now, whoever told you that?"

"That's the general word around here."

"Well, I'm almost seventeen. I suppose I can speak to whomever I please."

"And you please to speak to me?"

"I don't see anyone else around, do you?"

"Thanks a lot."

Mary inspected him discreetly. He *was* awfully handsome in a rugged sort of way, and he had changed during the past two months. He had filled out and developed some muscles. His skin was tanned now, making him look hale and hearty. His big cowboy hat sat rakishly atop his head, and his lopsided grin made him appear to be just a minute away from some devilry. But he had the nicest eyes—kind and gentle. "How old are you?" she asked.

"Almost nineteen." That was stretching it a bit, since he wouldn't be nineteen until December.

"Where are you from?"

"South of San Antonio. My folks are farmers."

"I'm from just north of San Antonio. A place called Crystal Creek."

"I know." He grinned at the look of surprise on her face.

"And how do you know that?"

"Well, I didn't exactly know the name of the place, but I knew you were from south of here. First day I saw you, someone told me."

"I'm not sure how I feel about having my name bandied about by the cowboys."

Hank chuckled. "Don't reckon it matters how you feel 'cause fellows are just naturally gonna talk about a pretty girl. How's school?"

"It's okay," she said flippantly, hoping the flush of pleasure she felt over hearing him say she was pretty wasn't evident to him. "I'm sure not going to shed any tears when I graduate."

"What do you study in a place like that?"

"Lots of things. English literature, history, etiquette, business skills."

"Why do you want so much schooling, anyway? You'll just be getting married and having babies one of these days. Don't need a whole heap of schooling for that."

Mary's dark eyes flashed. "I won't be getting married anytime soon, not for years and years. Women have other choices now."

A lopsided grin creased his face. "For instance?"

Mary pulled herself up to her full height of five foot three. "For instance, any business worth its name needs a stenographer and a bookkeeper. I could be either."

"Do tell. You gonna work in an office?"

"I might."

"With a bunch of men?"

"Something wrong with that?"

"Oh, I don't know. Businessmen don't always mind their manners or their language. Working alongside 'em just doesn't seem very ladylike to me."

"What's 'ladylike'? Pouring tea? We live in very modern times. A lady can do anything she pleases now, Mr. . . ."

"Travis."

"Mr. Travis."

"You can call me Hank."

"Well . . . thank you *so* much."

Grinning, Hank took a few steps toward her but was careful not to get too close. He nonchalantly reached into his shirt pocket and withdrew a pouch of tobacco and a paper. He had gotten good at rolling cigarettes by now. "Mind if I smoke?"

"No. As a matter of fact, I once smoked a cigarette." She once had taken two puffs of one when she was visiting Harriet's parents' house.

Hank stared at her in disbelief. "You?"

"Yes. In Fort Worth, a lot of women smoke. At least some do."

"That's disgusting."

"But perfectly all right for you men?"

"No woman should have the right to smoke."

Mary smiled. "Oh, before long, women are going to have the right to do a lot more than smoke."

"Like what?"

"Vote, for one thing."

Hank laughed. "It'll be years before you can vote, even if the law allowed."

"But when I'm twenty-one, I want that right. I want my life to be very different from my mother's."

Funny, Hank thought. Those were exactly his sentiments about his life as compared to his father's. He propped a foot on the first rung of the corral fence and pushed back his hat with his thumb, the way he'd seen the other cowhands do. He hoped he was giving Mary the impression that conversing with a pretty girl was nothing new to him. He was enjoying the hell out of this, mainly because he simply liked looking at her.

"How long have you been a cowboy?" she asked.

"Not long."

"Like it?"

He shrugged. "Reckon it'll do till I can get to the oil fields."

"Seems to me there are some oil fields right around here."

"I'm going to Oklahoma. Maybe even California," Hank said with a little bravado.

"Do tell. What do you know about drilling for oil?"

"Not much, but I'm a quick learner."

Mary's eyes twinkled merrily. "At least you aren't a liar. I'll be seeing you, Hank."

"Maybe you'd best not. I don't want to get fired."

"I'll see what I can do about that." She strode off toward the house.

Hank chuckled. *Hell,* he thought. *She isn't snooty. She's just feisty.* Having never known a feisty woman, he was even more enchanted with her than before.

MARY ENTERED the main house through the kitchen door and smiled at Lola, the woman who cooked for her uncle. She then headed to Duncan's office, a big Spartan room on the other side of the house. Knocking lightly on the door, she waited for a summons, then entered the room—a purely masculine retreat that smelled of old leather and stale tobacco.

Duncan looked up from his desk. "Well, hello, dear. What can I do for you?"

"There's a young cowboy working for you who's about my age. I'd appreciate it if you'd allow us to become friends." Actually, Mary had every intention of cultivating a friendship with Hank Travis, whether her uncle approved or not. It would just be nicer if she didn't have to do it covertly.

Duncan frowned. "Travis?"

"Yes."

"What on earth would a lady like you have to talk about with a common cowhand?"

"Besides being a lady, I'm a person. I'm also almost seventeen and he's...somewhere near that. I would simply like someone my own age to talk to once in a while. Except for the month I'll spend with Mama and the boys, I see nothing for me this summer but keeping my nose in a book."

Duncan pondered that. He supposed it was lonely for Mary Margaret on the ranch. And he thought about Hank Travis. He knew just about everything there was to know about the cowhand, something that would have astonished Hank to no end. Nice kid from all he'd been able to gather, but he felt so responsible for his niece. He wished he knew more about the ways of young people these days. From what he'd seen, they had a hell of a lot more freedom than he and his brothers had when they were in their teens. This parenting business was damned hard work.

"I...I don't see anything wrong with passing the time of day with him *occasionally*," he finally said. "Just friendly-like, you understand."

"Of course, Duncan. That's all I'm asking for."

"No long walks in the moonlight or anything like that."

"Good heavens, no!" Mary appeared to be shocked, but she wasn't . . . not even a little bit. She supposed it wasn't too farfetched to believe she and Hank Travis might someday take a walk in the moonlight. It was a nice thought.

"And be careful. We can't have the other men thinking Travis is getting any special consideration."

"No one will have any cause to complain, I assure you." Rounding the desk, she dropped a light kiss on his cheek. "Thank you."

After leaving her uncle's office, Mary again crossed the house and went out the back door. Pausing on the veranda, she lifted a hand to shade her eyes from the sun and looked toward the corral. Hank was still there, so she tripped down the steps and made her way toward the fence. It was a few minutes before he spotted her. When he did, he looked to the left, to the right, then at her. His eyes were wary.

She smiled. "You may feel free to speak to me anytime you please."

"You sure?"

"Positive. I spoke to my uncle."

"You mean . . . you actually asked him if it was all right for us to talk to each other?" he asked with a little laugh.

"Yes."

"Why?"

"Because I wanted to, silly."

"Well...thanks." Hank didn't think anything had ever pleased him so much.

"I'll be seeing you, Hank." With a smile, Mary turned and walked back to the house.

Hank grinned as he watched her cross the yard. Talking to Mary was a heap sight different from talking to Billie Jean. With Billie Jean he'd often felt as if he was engaged in some kind of game. She had been a great one for lowered eyes and pouts. Coquettish, he supposed was the word for it. Try as he might, he couldn't imagine Mary ever pouting.

One thing was for sure. A pretty girl could sure make an otherwise sensible fellow feel foolish.

"I'VE SEEN YOU talking to Mary Margaret, Hank," Jed said to him a few days later. "You'd better stop that if you want to keep this job."

"It's all right," Hank assured him. "She spoke to her uncle, and he said he didn't mind us talking to each other now and then."

Jed's eyes narrowed. "How come it's all right for you to talk to her and none of the rest of us can?"

"Guess you'd have to ask Mr. MacGregor that."

"And how come Mary Margaret finds you so much more interestin' than the rest of us?"

"Don't know," Hank said with a twinkle in his eye. "Guess she doesn't like old men like you, Jed."

HANK USUALLY RAN into Jimmy Blue when he had reason to be in Slaterton, and the geologist had started him vacillating on Oklahoma. "Sure, there's a lot of play going on up there now, Hank," Jimmy said on this particular night, "but there are oilers stumbling all over one another in Oklahoma. I'm telling you—and someday I'll be able to say I told you so—West Texas is the mother lode. It could all start right under the YH Ranch...if only Mac-Gregor wasn't so goddamned stubborn."

Every time Hank talked to Jimmy, he got a gut feeling that maybe his future wasn't in Oklahoma after all. What if he was already where he was supposed to be?

Then one night he had a dream, and he saw it—a wooden rig pumping black gold—and it was pumping it smack in the middle of YH Ranch. He woke with a start, excitement coursing through him. Jimmy was right! The oil was there. But how were they going to convince Duncan MacGregor of that?

Hank kept his dreams or visions or whatever they were to himself, lest folks think him teched in the head. But he had been having them all his life. And the things he saw always came to pass. It was eerie in a way. Scary, too. He was afraid there was something wrong with his brain. As odd as it was, he thought Mary might be the one person on the face of the earth whom he could tell about his dreams and not have her laugh hysterically. The brain inside that pretty head of hers seemed receptive to every weird idea that came down the road.

But he didn't say a word, chiefly because he feared ruining what he knew was a fragile relationship. A man who "saw" things before they came to pass might be too much for even Mary.

IN SOME WAYS, that was the most wonderful summer of Hank's young life. He loved listening to Jimmy talk, just as he loved absorbing more and more knowledge about the business he was convinced would form part of his future.

And there was Mary. They didn't see as much of each other as Hank would have liked, but when work kept him close to the main house, she made a point of coming out to talk to him, and each time she did, he felt his affection for her growing. He didn't welcome the emotion by any means, feeling sure he knew what it would lead to, but he couldn't seem to help himself. There was just something about Mary. Oh, she had a lot of crazy ideas and far more spunk than a girl was supposed to have, but he liked her, even if they didn't always see eye to eye.

"I read a book I probably wasn't supposed to read," she told him on one occasion.

"Oh? Why did you read it if you weren't supposed to?"

Mary shot him a look of the utmost disgust. "Precisely for that reason. Its title was *Women in the Nineteenth Century*."

"This is the twentieth, in case you'd forgotten."

"It was published more than sixty years ago. Even then there were those who said women should be allowed to vote. It's a disgrace that nothing's been done in all that time."

"Why do you want that, Mary? The vote. Why is it so important to you females?"

"Because it's there, and we don't have it. You wouldn't understand."

Hank chuckled. "That's what you say every time you run out of arguments."

She then slipped into a pensive mood. "I'm going to be leaving next week, going to visit my family."

"That's right. I'd forgotten." Hank suddenly felt blue. "How long will you be gone?"

"About a month, I guess."

That sounded like an eternity. "Are you looking forward to it?"

She shrugged. "Well, I want to see Mama, of course, but the farm is so boring. I'm out of touch with the people I went to school with. Funny, I used to think this ranch was boring, too, but now I have you, and that makes a difference. You *are* my friend, aren't you, Hank?"

"Forever, Mary."

The smile she gave him made Hank's insides melt like ice on an August day.

The weeks she spent visiting her family seemed an eternity to him. As summer inched toward September, he wondered how he was going to feel when she went back to the academy.

Too soon he found out. He existed in a blue funk for days after she left. It wasn't that they had ever spent a lot of time together, but as long as she was on the ranch, there always was a *chance* he would see her and talk with her.

He knew it was silly to spend so much time thinking about her. They were from different worlds. She went to a fancy school in a big city. She had all sorts of things she wanted to do when she graduated—get a job in an office, campaign for the vote for women. *Remember Billie Jean,* he cautioned himself over and over again. The day would come when Mary would leave for good, and didn't he have his own dreams?

Yet none of his sensible arguments did much good. He lived for Christmas and the sight of Mary.

VERY EARLY in his stay at the YH, Hank had decided that Saturday nights in Slaterton were not a good idea. He always spent more money there than he should, and he always felt awful the next morning. It was at Gracie's that he'd surrendered his virginity, and that experience had called him back too many times. Eventually, however, good sense had tempered his lust. So little by little he began giving those nights on the town a wide berth and spending them with Jimmy in his pigeonhole of an office at Holt Petroleum. Tonight he found the geologist seated at his desk, drawing something in the kind of tablet schoolchildren used.

"What'cha doin'?" Hank asked.

"Hello, Hank. Sit down. I'm just figuring something in my head. Look at this." He tore out the piece of paper and shoved it across the desk.

Hank picked it up and studied it, frowning. "You're drawing pictures of houses?"

Jimmy leaned across the desk and tapped the paper with a pencil. "This is the Bruner place...and this is Ned Fairley's spread. Down here is the Rocking W. Holt's drilling there, and early indications are it's going to make a well. And up here in the middle of all this is YH Ranch."

"So?"

"So...there's a certified maxim in the oil business. If you want to find oil, get close to oil. And Duncan's about as close to it as a body can get."

Hank put the paper on the desk. "That oil's down there. I know it."

Jimmy grinned. "Oh? Where did you get your degree in geology?"

"I've just got a feeling." Since Jimmy was a scientist, Hank decided against telling him he knew it was there because he had seen it in a dream. Jimmy would think he was some kind of crazy, and there would go the friendship and Hank's chance to get into the oil business. "But you're wasting your time, Jimmy. Duncan's not gonna let you haul a rig out to the YH...no way, no how."

"I'm going to tell you something, Hank. This unlovely country has just gone through a year of drought. Now out here, droughts don't last only a year. They last for years and years. I've heard of some that lasted six years. They just about kill the ranchers. One more dry spring, and Duncan's just apt to start hurting." Jimmy sat back in his chair and tapped his mouth with the pencil. "I'm wondering. Aren't you and that niece of his kinda friendly?"

"Little bit."

"Maybe you could talk to her, and she would talk to him."

"Maybe, but I still don't think it's gonna do any good. Besides, Mary's at school and won't be home until Christmas."

"Holt's waited this long. I'm sure we can wait until Christmas."

"Don't know as I'll see her much. Her mother and brothers are coming up for the holiday, and she only has two weeks."

"Next summer, then. Like I said, we can wait." Jimmy shoved himself out of the chair. "Want to go get some supper at Barney's?"

"Might as well," Hank said, also standing. He picked up the paper from the desk. "Mind if I have this?"

"Help yourself, but why do you want it?"

"It's something I can show Mary when she comes home." Hank carefully folded the paper, placed it in his shirt pocket and followed Jimmy out of the office.

As it turned out, Hank did not have to wait until Christmas to see Mary again. He was mending a fence near the main house one warm Saturday morning in early November when a buggy—a carriage was more like it—drove through the gate and up to the house. Before his startled eyes, Mary hopped out and almost ran to the porch. She was carrying two pieces of luggage. Behind her came the driver, a large bosomed, corseted woman of about forty. Even from afar, Hank could see that both Mary and the woman were quite angry.

His curiosity ran rampant. Perhaps twenty minutes passed before the older woman emerged from the house with Duncan hard on her heels. They paused in the middle of the veranda, obviously engaged in an argument. Finally the woman returned to the carriage and drove off. Duncan went back inside and slammed the front door with more force than was necessary. Hank was surprised the fancy stained glass pane didn't shatter.

More than curiosity assailed him. His heart pounded with excitement over knowing she was here, on the premises, and that was just about the dumbest thing he could think of. It irritated him that he so easily imagined more about their relationship than actually existed.

Still, he found it almost impossible to concentrate on the task at hand, not that fence mending required a great deal of concentration or thought. Nevertheless, he dawdled, prolonging the job as much as possible. He kept watching the house, hoping for the sight of Mary and wondering what had brought her home. It was late afternoon before he found out.

The men were straggling toward the bunkhouse, in from their various chores and anticipating supper. Hank was in the toolshed, putting away his equipment, when he heard that soft, melodious voice.

"Hello."

He turned. "Hello." She was so pretty she made him ache. "What brings you home?"

Her dark eyes flashed. "I've been expelled."

Hank's mouth dropped. "Expelled? From the academy?"

"Now what else would I have been expelled from?" There was a mixture of anger and sadness in her voice.

"Mary! What happened?"

"It's a very long story."

At that moment the chuck cook's bell clanged. Hank was starved, just as all the cowboys were at the end of the day. "I...really need supper," he said reluctantly, "but I want to know what happened."

"Then meet me on the front porch sometime around seven."

"But...won't your uncle...."

Mary interrupted him. "I am so sick of being told what I can and cannot do! Whom I can and cannot see! What I am and am not supposed to think! I'm seventeen! Meet me." With a swish of her skirts, she turned and went back to the house.

SUPPER in the bunkhouse was normally a leisurely affair that went on for an hour or more. Then the men played cards or sat around and swapped yarns. Hank was more of an observer than a participant, for he wasn't a card player, and he had no cowboying yarns to tell. But he always enjoyed the winding down at the end of the day, and was grateful for the times he could stay in the bunkhouse instead of bedding down with the herd.

Tonight, however, he was restless. He waited until it was nearing seven, then slipped on his jacket and announced he was going for a walk, hoping all the while that no one would want to join him.

No one did. He went outside and paused to roll and light a cigarette before positioning himself against the trunk of a tall live oak, a spot that gave him a clear view of the front of the house. He was half-afraid that Mary might not show up at all, that Duncan might intervene. However, knowing Mary, she might climb out the window and shinny down one of the pillars if that happened.

Fortunately, that wasn't necessary. Hank had been standing by the tree perhaps fifteen minutes when the front door opened and she stepped out onto the veranda. Around her shoulders she wore a heavy shawl. Hank straightened and crossed the grounds.

"Hank?" Mary called.

"I'm here," he said, walking to the foot of the steps.

"Good. Let's sit here, shall we?" She sat on the top step and motioned for him to sit beside her.

"Are you sure this is all right?" he asked, casting a worried glance at the front door.

"Duncan and Matt are drinking brandy and playing cards. If they think about me at all, they'll assume I went to my room. Besides, Duncan doesn't care if I talk to you. He thinks you're a steadying influence on me.''

"How do you know that?''

"I heard him talking to Matt once.''

Hank wasn't sure how he felt about that. It made him sound so noble, and there were times when his thoughts about Mary were anything but noble. He sat down beside her. "So, what happened at the academy?''

Mary's face darkened. "It was so silly...so uncalled for. Harriet and I...oh, I told you about Harriet, didn't I? Last summer?''

He nodded.

"Well, it was Saturday, so Harriet and I went into town to go to the moving pictures. But there was a suffragette march right down the main street. There must have been two hundred or more women. Without thinking too much about it, I told Harriet we ought to join them. Before I knew it, there we were, right in the vanguard, marching down the street. One of the women handed me a placard. Oh, it was such fun and so exciting! But then the police showed up and started shoving everyone around. Men were standing on the sidewalk laughing at us. Then one of the policemen grabbed my arm really hard and called me 'girlie.' I was furious, so I hit him over the head with my placard, and since it was made out of wood, it rather stunned him a minute, I think.

"Anyway, I guess the police could tell Harriet and I were younger than the other women, and they wanted to know where we lived. We didn't tell them at first, but then they said they were taking us to jail, so we told them." Mary paused to sigh. "They marched us to the academy, and Miss Totten, the headmistress, said we were a disgrace to the school and expelled us right on the spot. She had her assistant take Harriet home, and she brought me here. I'll bet Harriet's parents are proud of her, but Duncan is mad at me. Not furious. Kind of exasperated...or disappointed. He says he won't let me go back to the academy, even if they'd take me. He says I'm apparently not learning anything useful and it's only right that my place be given to someone 'more deserving.' Isn't it strange? I hated the place most of the time I was there, but now that I know I can't go back, I think I'm going to miss it."

Her eyes were so downcast, her face so sad, that Hank had to restrain himself forcibly from reaching out and giving her shoulder a reassuring pat. "Oh, Mary," he said, slowly shaking his head. "I'm sorry."

"The women weren't harming anyone. They weren't unruly or interfering with traffic or anything like that. Ten thousand men could have marched down the street for one reason or another, and nothing would have happened." She fumed in silence a minute before adding, "I think what upset Miss Totten more than anything was the placard.''

"Because you hit the policeman with it?"

"No, not exactly. How was I to know what the silly thing said? Someone handed it to me, so I carried it."

"Well . . . what did it say?"

Mary looked at him sheepishly. "No ballots, no babies."

Hank gasped, then laughed as the picture of her formed in his mind. "You didn't!"

"I did. So, here I am—a failure at seventeen," she went on miserably. "I missed graduation by seven months. What am I to do with myself? I don't want to go back to Crystal Creek, but what is there for me to do here? I can't go to Fort Worth and get a job until I'm eighteen. Of course," she mused, apparently hitting on an idea, "I could lie about my age."

"Oh, Mary . . . why do you want to be such a squeaky wheel?"

She stared off into space. "I don't know, Hank. I just am. Always have been, and I don't guess I'll ever change. I'll never be a proper lady."

"Aw, that's not so. Why, I think you're just about the finest lady I've ever seen."

She looked at him, her eyes widening, and a small smile curved her mouth. "Do you really think so?"

"I do indeed."

"Thank you. That's very sweet. But I'm not sure I want to be one, not if it means staying home and playing the piano. Not if it means never doing anything exciting. You men have it so easy. You can do anything you want to do, be anything you have the gumption to be. It seems to me that women have to fight for everything they want." Abruptly she stood. "I . . . I guess I'd better go in now. No sense trying my uncle's patience too much in one day. I'll see you tomorrow, won't I?"

"I'm afraid not. I'll be out on the range the rest of the week."

"When you get back then. I'll be watching for you. I'll have precious little else to do, it seems. Good night, Hank. Thank you so much for listening to me."

Hank stood. "Thank *you* for talking to me."

She disappeared into the house. Hank stood on the veranda for a few minutes, staring at the closed door. She was as spirited as a colt. No man would ever put a rein on her. No one would even want to try. She'd probably scare the hell out of any man who got to know her well.

This was one time when he wished he could call up one of his visions at will. He'd like to see just what the future held in store for Mary. Was she destined to spend it alone, championing one cause after another? Or would she spend it as most girls did—married and a mother with a house to take care of? And would her husband take all the fire out of her?

A feeling as heavy as lead settled over him. He wondered if he was in love again. If so, he was sure it was the worst thing that had ever happened to him, worse even than Billie Jean's rejection. He sometimes went weeks without ever thinking of the aristocratic Miss Surratt, but he feared he'd spend the rest of his life pining away for Mary.

CHAPTER THREE

THREE DAYS before Christmas, Emma MacGregor arrived at the YH with Mary's three brothers in tow. Duncan had already written his sister-in-law about Mary's expulsion from the academy, so the reunion was not as warm as it might have been. Duncan and Emma held several closed-door sessions concerning "the problem of Mary Margaret."

Initially it was decided she would return to Crystal Creek with her mother and brothers, but Mary's ensuing wails of protest rang through the house. "I'm not going to go back to the farm!" she declared. "I'll kill myself first." After much arguing back and forth, Duncan and Emma again secluded themselves to put their heads together.

"Mary Margaret's always been such a headstrong girl," Emma said with a sigh. "Willful, I believe it's called. She should have been a boy."

Duncan snorted. "A boy with her spunk would probably be in a heap of trouble most of the time."

"I never could get her interested in cooking or sewing or keeping house. She much preferred being outside, pitching hay, swinging from trees or collecting...bugs." Emma shuddered in revulsion. "Duncan, no girl likes bugs, but Mary Margaret did. I thought she might make a good teacher since she was so curious about everything, but she declared she wanted to work in a business in a city. As much as I hate to admit it, I'm afraid my daughter isn't suited to be a farm wife."

"I'm inclined to agree. Just what she *is* suited for remains to be decided. However, since she seems determined to stay here, I think that might be the best course of action."

"You don't mind? She's such a handful."

Duncan smiled. "I don't mind. I can handle her. She's made a friend here, a young man named Hank Travis."

"A young man?"

"Now, Emma, don't go getting worried. I've kept an eye on them. They're only friends. Hank's a good young'un. Pretty levelheaded, seems to me. Yes, I just might have to call on that young man."

THE FOLLOWING DAY, Duncan went in search of Hank. He found him with a half dozen cowboys out in the northwest quadrant of the ranch. The rancher spent a few minutes studying the lad before he approached him. By this time, Hank sat a saddle as though born to it, and he had gained a lot of self-confidence. He got along well with the men, no small accomplishment since cowboys could be downright churlish about taking orders from someone they didn't respect. Duncan wondered if ranching looked any more appealing to the young man, or if he still longed for the oil fields of Oklahoma. Pity if he did. Duncan wouldn't have hesitated to offer the foreman's job to Hank if it had been available. It wasn't, but something else was. Nudging his horse's flank, he hailed the young cowboy.

Seeing the big boss, Hank respectfully touched the brim of his hat in greeting.

"'Mornin', Mr. MacGregor. Nice one, isn't it?"

"Beautiful," Duncan agreed. "Want to talk to you, son."

"Oh? Well, yes, sir."

"Matt's leaving us. Going to hire on with a big outfit farther west. Guess that means Jed'll be taking his place. I was wondering if you'd be interested in Jed's job."

Hank could honestly have said it was the last thing in the world he would have expected. And he wondered if by saying yes he would be putting himself in an awkward position. A couple of old-timers had quit since his arrival, and two fellows younger than himself had signed on, but he still was newer and younger than most of the men he worked with. He knew next to nothing about protocol on a ranch, but something warned him that the others might not take kindly to some fresh-faced kid off the farm giving them orders. "Well, sir...that's mighty nice of you, but...the other men might not like it."

"Then they can leave. But they won't. Most wouldn't take the job of assistant foreman if I doubled their pay. Don't want the responsibility. Do you?"

Hank had no idea why Duncan had singled him out, but he experienced a sense of satisfaction that he had. Of course it didn't change much, not really. Hank knew with certainty that his future was not in ranching. However, his present was. "Sure, I want it, Mr. MacGregor. Thanks."

Duncan wheeled his horse around and pointed it south, toward the big house. "You can call me Duncan now," he called as he rode off.

Duncan hoped he was doing the right thing. He'd noticed that the young cowboy seemed to have some kind of influence with Mary, at least to the extent that *anybody* had influence with his niece. Maybe Hank could temper her exuberance to some extent. Duncan realized that he himself would have to soften his formerly rigid stance about Mary and the cowhands. Hank would have to be allowed to visit in the big house. Just how that would work,

Duncan wasn't sure; he'd just have to play the cards as they were dealt.

He chuckled as he trotted toward home. Emma was right. That girl was a handful.

CHRISTMAS CAME and went; Emma and the boys returned home. Mary was so relieved to learn she wasn't being sent back to Crystal Creek that for weeks she was careful to make no waves, to be a pleasant, unobtrusive presence in the house. January arrived, the slowest part of the year. The cowboys mostly stayed close to the house, making repairs and passing the time as best they could, so Mary got to see more of Hank than she usually did. And now that he had been given Jed Purcell's job, he had even been invited inside the house a few times. Her uncle, to her everlasting surprise, seemed to recognize her need for the companionship of people her own age.

Winter finally blew itself out by the first of April, and still there was no rain. Mary could tell Duncan was worried, but he would be the last to admit it. Once she had heard her uncle refer to drought as a "soul-searing experience," and she was beginning to understand what he'd meant. The land looked so brown and dry and forlorn, and the grass was in deplorable condition. Hank said the men were worried to death about prairie fires, and inside the house, the cook and the maids grumbled constantly about the dust.

And the grit took its toll on Mary, too. On days when it was really bad, when the air was thick with the stuff, a tight knot would form in her throat, and she would be seized by fits of coughing. That so alarmed Duncan that he summoned a doctor who declared it was "dust fever" and gave her a bottle of molasseslike syrup that helped some. Fortunately, there weren't too many really bad days, though it irritated Mary no end that she ever felt unwell, for to her that was a sign of weakness.

She was extremely careful not to let Hank know anything about her illnesses. Always when she'd been forced to stay inside for a few days he would ask where she'd been, and always she would mumble something about a "mild spell," naturally leaving him to guess it had something to do with female problems.

The dry weather continued, but neither the dust nor the drought could prevent the local citizens from attending the county fair, least of all the people at the YH. It was the biggest event of the year for folks permanently starved for entertainment. Each year it got bigger and bigger, and this year was extra special. For one thing, there would be a Ferris wheel, the first one ever in that part of the country. And as if that weren't enough, a troupe of barnstorming pilots was going to be on hand to perform a flying exhibition. The posters that were hung all over town called it "The Show of Shows." And after the performance, the advertisements said, anyone with two dollars who wanted to would be taken up for a ride.

"Will you let Hank take me to the fair, Duncan?" Mary asked in her sweetest voice.

"I don't suppose there'll be anything wrong with that. Just stay at the fairgrounds. Don't go wandering off."

"We won't."

"We can all meet at the fireworks display after sundown."

Mary was so relieved that Duncan didn't insist she go with him. It would be easy to slip away from Hank for a little while. She wished she could let him in on her plans, but in some respects he was as bad as Duncan when it came to "protecting" her. So she planned to tell Hank she wanted to go to the pie judging, something no fellow would admit to having an interest in, and he'd no doubt want to hang around the livestock barns, a smelly prospect at best. No one would even miss her. Smiling secretively, she patted the two dollars she had tucked away in her shirtwaist. No one would give her the permission, but she *was* going to fly. It was the most exciting thing she could think of.

WHEN MARY AND HANK arrived at the fairgrounds, the place was already teeming with people. For a time they strolled the area, gawking at display booths and munching on cotton candy. There was a hopelessly long line at the Ferris wheel, so that had to wait. After a while, as Mary had expected, Hank suggested the livestock barns. "Come on," he urged. "The YH has a couple of steers entered."

"I see more cattle than I want to every day of my life," she said. "You go on. I think I'm just going to wander around and look at everything."

"We'll get separated."

"No, we won't. I'll find you."

Hank argued with her for a minute, but that was a useless endeavor. In the end she told him she was going to the food judging and afterward would come to the livestock barns. He accepted that. Mary watched until he was swallowed up in the crowd; then she hurried purposefully away.

The flying exhibition was being held in an open field adjacent to the fairgrounds. Quite a crowd had gathered to see the daring young eagles put on a show with their machines. Three aeroplanes were parked in the field—two Wrights and a Farman. Mary knew that because the posters advertising the exhibition had given the names of the planes. To her inexperienced eye, the Wrights looked a little sturdier than the Farman.

Then the aviators walked out on the field, swaggering slightly and pretending they weren't enjoying every second of the oohs and aahs of the crowd. They were the real-life heroes of their day, and they knew it. They climbed into their planes and were airborne within minutes. The planes glided and cavorted to the astonished gasps of the audience, and when they landed, it was to thunderous applause.

One of the pilots sauntered up and down in front of the spectators. "All right, folks, who wants to go up? Two dollars. That's not much for the thrill of a lifetime."

Mary was the only one who stepped forward. She thrust her two dollars into the pilot's hand. "I do, sir. I want to go up."

"You, miss? How old are you?"

"Eighteen," she fibbed.

"Are your parents with you?"

"I said I'm eighteen. I no longer have to have my parents' permission for every little thing I do."

The pilot still seemed doubtful, but the little lady had spunk. None of these other yokels would risk going up. "All right, Miss..."

"MacGregor."

"Miss MacGregor, I'll be honored to take you for your first aeroplane ride. Please come with me."

THE LIVESTOCK JUDGING had begun to pall for
Hank, so he decided to go in search of Mary. But a
subsequent check of all the booths where food was
being judged did not turn up a sight of her. He
thoroughly combed the fairgrounds but couldn't
find her. He had about decided to check their team
and wagon to see if she was resting there when he
heard the sound of applause. Looking in the direction of the noise, he spotted an aeroplane glide to
a landing in an open field. A huge crowd was
watching, so he sauntered over to join them.

"What's going on?" he asked one of the spectators.

"A little lady went up in that thing with the pilot," the man said, chuckling.

"A lady?"

"Yep. She gave him two dollars, and he took her
up."

"Wh-who was it?"

"Don't know. Just a pretty little thing with dark
hair."

Hank was almost afraid to watch. He could think
of only one "little lady" with dark hair within a
radius of a hundred miles who would do such a
stupid thing.

The plane came to a stop in front of the crowd.
The pilot hopped down and held out his hand to his
passenger. Sure enough, before Hank's incredu-
lous eyes, Mary Margaret MacGregor's feet

touched the ground. The crowd applauded her nerve. He wanted to choke her.

"What in the hell do you think you're doing?" he gasped, grabbing her arm as she rejoined the spectators.

"Oh, Hank." Her face with flushed with excitement. "I've just had the most glorious experience."

"Have you lost your mind? You could have been killed in that crate!"

She pinched her lips together. "I suppose I could have. And I could be killed on a train... or by a runaway horse and buggy. Or by some horrible disease. But I haven't been."

Hank's stomach was jumping up and down as if it were filled with toads. All the "what ifs" came to mind. God, how could anyone be so... so headstrong?

Then he thought of something else. Taking her by the shoulders, he turned her around to face him. "Mary, you can't ever let Duncan know you took an aeroplane ride today. He would kill me. I was supposed to be looking after you."

Her eyes blazed. "Looking after me? What am I—a baby in a carriage, a dog on a leash? I can look after myself." Suddenly her mood changed completely. She took his hands from her shoulders and gave them a shake. "Oh, Hank, I wish you could have been with me! You can *feel* it!"

"Feel what?"

"The very air that holds you up there. You really can feel it." Her eyes wandered to the sky. "There's such a sense of freedom in the sky. I wonder if a woman will fly an aeroplane someday."

"Oh, of course not, Mary," he scoffed. "Why would one even want to?"

"Because it's such...well, it's such...an *adventure*." Her eyes turned dreamy. "Maybe I won't go to the city and work in a business office, after all. Maybe I'll go someplace where I can learn to fly an aeroplane and be world-famous. Just thinking about it makes being a stenographer sound very dull in comparison."

Hank sighed and wondered if she would actually do that given the chance. Adventure. He himself sought adventure in the form of the oil fields, but the things Mary wanted seemed so outrageous, so pie-in-the-sky. "Ah, Mary," he said, "the world's just not big enough for the likes of you."

DUNCAN NEVER LEARNED about the plane ride at the fair, to Hank's everlasting relief. Had he, he never would have let his niece spend so much time with the young cowboy, who could control her no more than he could.

So, with warmer weather, Mary and Hank could once again sit and talk on the porch. She often wondered what on earth she would do if Hank wasn't around. She found herself looking forward to their after-supper chats. They had become the high points of her days, and it amazed her that she and Hank never ran out of things to talk about.

One evening, when she came out after supper, she found him seated on one of the porch chairs, studying something in the soft amber glow of the gaslights that flanked the front door.

"What are you reading?" she asked, taking a chair beside him.

"Just an old map Jimmy drew for me a while back."

"A map? What kind of map?"

"Of this area around here, at least the way a geologist looks at it."

"May I see it?"

"Sure." Hank handed her the piece of paper. He had handled it so much it was dog-eared.

Mary studied it a minute, then frowned. "This isn't a map. It's a drawing of some houses ... not a very good one, either. What are all these black circles under the houses?"

"Pools of oil ... at least, Jimmy thinks so. See ... this is the Bruner place, and this house represents the Fairley spread, and this over here is the Rocking W."

"So what's this one?"

"The YH."

Mary continued poring over the paper, while Hank was content to sit with his arms crossed behind his head and stare out into the dark prairie night. He couldn't imagine what a girl would find so interesting about a geologist's scribblings.

"Hank?" she finally said.

"Hmm?"

"I don't know much about this, but I was wondering..." She shoved the paper under his nose and tapped it with a fingertip. "Mr. Bruner and Mr. Fairley both have wells on their property that are bringing oil out of the ground."

"Right."

"Well, when that oil comes up, what's to keep the oil that's supposed to be under the YH from just sort of sliding over and taking its place? Then wouldn't it be Mr. Bruner's and Mr. Fairley's oil?"

Hank simply stared at her a minute, then he grabbed the paper and studied it a bit longer. "Good Lord, Mary. I don't know, but... I think you might be a genius!" Folding the paper and stuffing it in his pocket, he jumped off the porch.

"Where are you going?" Mary cried, getting to her feet.

"To find Jimmy," he called over his shoulder.

"On foot? Take a horse... or one of the wagons."

"It's not that far, and I don't want to take the time to saddle a horse or hitch a wagon. I'll talk to you later, Mary." He was off in a trot.

"WHAT DO YOU THINK, Jimmy? Could she be right?"

Jimmy rubbed his chin thoughtfully. "I'm not sure, but given the nature of oil, the way it moves around in the reservoir... Tell you what, Hank. In the morning I'll go to Fort Worth and find a library. A whole lot of stuff has been discovered since I was in school. If she's right, we just might have ourselves a calling card. Yes, sir, this might be something old Duncan would be interested in hearing. Come and see me after supper tomorrow night."

The next day passed on leaden feet for Hank. He ate supper hastily that night, and because he was anxious to hear what Jimmy had found out, he took the time to saddle a horse for the trip into town. Once he arrived at Holt's camp, he discovered that his friend had indeed stumbled onto new information.

"Your girlfriend was on the right track, Hank," Jimmy told him. "It's all technical jargon, but I've worked up a little speech that a layman can understand... I think. All we've got to do is get Duncan to hear it."

"You know...Jed told me Duncan's talking about culling the herd. Maybe this drought has him hurting. Come on back to the ranch with me, Jimmy. I'll talk to Mary. She's probably wondering where in the devil I am since I talk to her most evenings."

"Let me go get a buggy."

Once back at the YH, Hank hopped up on the veranda of the main house, knocked on the door and was relieved to see Mary herself open it.

"I was wondering where you were," she said, glancing at Jimmy with curiosity.

"Jimmy, this is Mary. Mary, my friend, Jimmy Blue."

"Pleased to meet you, ma'am."

"Likewise."

"Er...Mary, we were wondering if we can have a few minutes of your uncle's time. We won't be long."

Mary shrugged. "Can't imagine why not. He's not doing much of anything, just drinking his brandy and reading the newspaper. Come in."

Hank and Jimmy exchanged an anxious glance before stepping into the foyer. "This way," Mary said, and led them into the living room. Duncan was seated in one of the big leather easy chairs that flanked the fireplace, his head buried inside a newspaper. He did not immediately see the trio standing at the threshold. Mary cleared her throat to get his attention.

"Duncan, Hank and his friend would like to have a word with you."

Duncan's head came up. Seeing the two men, he closed the paper and laid it on the floor next to the chair, then stood. "Travis? What can I do for you?"

"Duncan, this is Jimmy Blue. He has something he wants to tell you."

Jimmy crossed the room and shook the rancher's hand. "I'd appreciate just a few minutes of your time, Mr. MacGregor."

"Don't I know you from somewhere, young man?"

"Possibly, sir. I'm a geologist. I work for Elver Holt."

"Holt?" Duncan scowled. "If this is about drilling on my land, my answer's the same as it's always been. No."

"Sir, I've come across new information that might make you change your mind."

"I doubt that," Duncan said with a grunt, "but since you're here, I might as well hear you out. Just make it short and sweet. Both of you have a seat."

Mary stayed in the background, but she didn't leave the room. Surprisingly, her uncle didn't ask her to. Normally she was expected to disappear when he talked business.

Once Hank and Jimmy were seated, Duncan gave them his full attention. Jimmy began to speak. "Now, Mr. MacGregor, you know that there are producing oil wells surrounding your property, so we know we've hit a previously undiscovered reservoir. Elver Holt is quite aware of how you feel about your land and your concerns over what oil people might do to it. But a drilling operation needn't interfere with ranching, and quite frankly, sir, you're robbing yourself by not bringing your oil to the surface, because it belongs to you whether you want it or not."

"I'm not following you, young man."

"You see, in the United States, unlike most countries in the world, ownership of subsurface minerals is vested in whoever owns the surface. But in the case of oil, property rights are a little different. That's because petroleum is what the books call a fugacious substance."

"A what?"

"That means it doesn't stay put. It shifts around in the reservoir as conditions in the reservoir change. Obviously, those wells surrounding you are disturbing the reservoir when they pump oil to the surface. You own property you can't fence in, and tomorrow it may shift and lie under your neighbor's property." Jimmy took a deep breath. "You put two straws down either side of a glass of water and suck...well, you're gonna get what's in the middle, too, whether there's a straw there or not."

That got Duncan's attention because he was a very proprietary man. His brows knitted, but he said nothing, so Jimmy felt encouraged enough to continue. "Oil production is largely governed by the law of capture. Whoever brings it to the surface owns it, regardless of where the oil originally was located."

Duncan mulled that over for a few seconds before saying, "Are you telling me that all those wells ringing my property are sucking up oil from under the YH?"

"It's entirely possible, sir. Of course they haven't been in production all that long, but eventually other people might get rich off something that actually belongs to you. Now those other wells are not big producers, but...well, sir, let me put it this way. We've found a couple of baby kittens, so somewhere nearby is the mama cat."

Bull's eye! Hank thought. He could see it in the expression on the rancher's face.

Again Duncan fell silent. Hank could almost see the wheels in his head turning. Finally he said, "I don't know anything that galls me more than having someone take something that's rightfully mine. I'd rather lose half my herd to disease than one cow to a rustler. Have Elver come out to see me."

Hank expelled his breath; Jimmy's shoulders sagged slightly as relief engulfed him. They both stood. "Thank you, Mr. MacGregor. I'm sure he'll be out tomorrow."

"I'll be waiting."

After a few more pleasantries were exchanged, Hank and Jimmy beat a hasty retreat. They could hardly wait to get out of there. Out on the porch, they restrained their glee, lest it could be heard inside the house. "You're a genius, Jimmy," Hank said in admiration.

"I *was* pretty magnificent, wasn't I? But I never would have thought of it if you hadn't brought it up in the first place. Old Elver's liable to give me a fat bonus for this, and I'll gladly share it with you, friend."

"Listen, Jimmy, I want to buy into this well. I want a share of it."

"Hell, we don't even have a lease yet. Duncan might sleep on it and decide the lease payment isn't worth the bother."

"You saw the look on his face. Holt will get that lease, and I want to be a player. I don't have a lot of money, but I haven't spent hardly anything this past year. I've got maybe three hundred dollars, and I'll give you every cent of it."

"Well, I don't know. Elver usually goes for the big-money guys when he's looking for investors, but... Oh, hell, when I tell him what you did, he'll let you in. I'm sure of it. And listen, this is only the beginning for us. Someday you and I are going to drill our own well."

Wildcatting? Hank had yet to even work on a rig. "You mean . . . be independents?"

"Yes, sir, Hank, I think you and I just feathered our nests handsomely."

They heard a sound behind them. Turning, the men found Mary glaring at them furiously. "You're welcome," she said sourly.

"Huh?" Hank asked.

"You two *brilliant* gentlemen have been so busy congratulating each other you seem to have forgotten just who it was who came up with the slipping and sliding oil in the first place."

"Oh . . . sorry, Mary. Thanks. Thanks a lot."

"Yes, ma'am," Jimmy said contritely. "I sure do thank you."

She folded her arms under her breasts. "And I want in on it, too."

"Huh?" Hank and Jimmy chorused.

"You heard me."

Hank took a couple of steps toward her. "Mary, are you talking about investing in the well?"

"Something like that. I have two hundred dollars that will come to me on my eighteenth birthday. Duncan's in charge of it, but if I plead my heart out, he'll let me have it now. I'll give it to you, Hank, and we can become partners."

Hank and Jimmy exchanged amused glances, then turned back to Mary.

"The well could come up dry," Hank reminded her, though he was sure it wouldn't.

"I know. Then we'll all lose. Ah, but if we hit oil, we'll all be rich."

Hank stared at her in admiration. "You're a gambler!" he exclaimed.

"Maybe. But it was *my* idea in the first place, and I want in on it."

"It's commerce, dammit, and no woman belongs in—" The frosty look he received caused Hank to drop the sentence. He had seen that unyielding expression many times. Turning to Jimmy, he said, "Might as well let her, friend...unless you have a peculiar fondness for squabbling with mean, stubborn females."

"Perish the thought!" Jimmy said in exaggerated horror. "Now if you two will excuse me, I've got to go find Elver. I hope he doesn't kiss me."

As Jimmy rode away in the buggy, Mary slid to Hank's side. Touching him on the arm, she said, "Isn't this exciting, Hank? This summer is going to be so much fun! If that well comes in, we'll both have money and can do anything we want. You won't have to be a cowboy anymore if you don't want, and I can go to Fort Worth and have a career. That is, if that's what we want when the time comes."

"You havin' second thoughts about being a fancy career woman?"

"I don't know. Are you having second thoughts about Oklahoma?"

"I don't know that, either. But I do know I don't want to be a cowboy the rest of my life."

Her grip on his arm tightened. "You won't have to be if our well comes in."

Our well. There was something about that *our* that caused his stomach muscles to tighten. It sounded great, but he wasn't a fool. They were friends, and that was all they'd ever be.

Later, Hank couldn't remember what he had said to her, or if he'd said anything. At the time he had been too preoccupied with the sight of her long, slender fingers with their perfect oval nails against the sleeve of his rough denim shirt. His own hands were brown and callused, and their nails were ragged and unclean, a cowpoke's hands. Their hands, more than anything, symbolized to Hank the world that lay between them.

CHAPTER FOUR

THE WELL on the MacGregor ranch generated a lot of interest, chiefly because the local citizens were acutely aware of Duncan's feelings about the oil business. What, they wondered, could have made him change his mind? Elver Holt must have done some fast talking. To Duncan's dismay, people would come out from town with folding chairs and camp stools, then sit around the ranch's grounds like spectators at a sporting event. One enterprising youngster of about twelve set up a lemonade stand and did a thriving business.

Mary could scarcely contain her excitement that summer of 1913. So much happened so fast. From the day the Holt crew showed up at the ranch to "make hole," she couldn't keep away from the well site, though she had been warned time and time again by Duncan to stay far from those oilers.

Hank was almost as insistent. "Just keep your distance, Mary," he told her. "They have the foulest mouths of any group I ever heard."

"Fiddlesticks. It's probably nothing I haven't heard before."

Hank looked startled. "If you've heard that kind of talk, you've been mixing with the wrong people."

"At Mayberry Academy? Hardly."

"So where did you hear that kind of talk?"

"Oh, I was just teasing. I can't stay away, Hank. I just can't."

And she noticed that he spent every minute he could at the site, too, watching and learning. It occurred to her that if they made any money off the well, Hank would be leaving, would maybe hie himself on up to Oklahoma as he had originally intended. It was so odd. As a child she'd had many friends and had taken them for granted. Since leaving Crystal Creek, however, she'd had only two—Harriet and Hank. Harriet was out of her life for good, she guessed. Mr. Warren had decided that Mayberry Academy was too backward for his bright daughter and had sent Harriet to a school near Boston. Mary hadn't had a letter from her for months. If Hank left, too... The thought was utterly depressing.

So she quickly shook it off. Never would she depend on any one person for her personal well-being. She'd miss Hank horribly for a while, of course, but it would pass. She had a future ahead of her, and with money that future would be infinitely easier.

But as Hank constantly reminded her, together they owned exactly two percent of the well, so it was going to have to be one sweet producer to net the two of them very much money.

MacGregor Number One, as the well was called, became reality in June. The day had been cloudy, but without rain. Then in late afternoon, the sun suddenly broke below the edge of the clouds. "A good omen," Mary said to Hank and Jimmy as the three of them stood on the periphery of all the activity.

There had been a lot of it all day, as the crew neared the depth Jimmy had established as more or less the "pay zone." Now everything was eerily quiet. One of the roughnecks knelt on the ground beside the flow pipe. "We've got a good blow of air," he called. "And it's beginning to stink." A minute passed, and no one moved. "This is the real thing," the veteran roughneck said.

"Douse all cigarettes! Shut 'er down, and everybody stand back," the driller yelled, and the men all scampered off the derrick floor.

The well began to make noise, first a whisper, then a soft, throaty roar that coughed. The excitement in the air was almost tangible. Mary moved closer to Hank, and he unconsciously slipped his arm around her waist.

The coughing became louder and more persistent. At first there was a little trickle of drilling mud, then a great belch of mud, gravel, gas and oil. Suddenly a thick column of green-black oil gushed out of the pipe and across the mud pit. The roar from the pipe drowned out the whoops and yells of the people at the site. The roughnecks rushed forward to bring the gusher under control.

"Oh, Hank, isn't it extraordinary!" Mary cried.

"That it is." He wouldn't have been able to describe the feeling that swept through him. He only knew that a man could spend an entire lifetime ranching or farming or doing any number of things and not have anything half so thrilling happen to him. And if he'd ever had doubts before, he no longer did. *This* was what he wanted to spend his life doing.

Suddenly Mary pivoted and headed for the house. "Where're you going?" Hank called after her.

"To tell Duncan," she called back, not slowing down. Mary was smiling from ear to ear, eager to see the expression on her uncle's face. Duncan had staunchly declared a lack of real interest in the well. After all, he'd said, he had no money tied up in the thing. The whole affair was strictly a business arrangement, not an emotional one, and he had studiously avoided joining the spectators who gathered at the well site almost daily.

Mary found him in his office. He looked up when she entered and smiled. "Hello, my dear. What can I do for you?"

"Duncan," she said, "I don't think you're going to have to worry about this ol' drought anymore."

IT WAS DECIDED that there should be a MacGregor Number Two, and Hank and Mary were asked if they wanted to invest in it again. Mary unhesitatingly sank her earnings from the first well into the second, but for Hank it was an agonizing decision. He had money now—not great riches, but far more than he'd ever had before. But in the end, the thought of a larger percentage, *real* money was too irresistible. Hadn't he seen the oil down there? He convinced himself it wasn't even much of a gamble.

When the second well also came in, an even better producer than the first, Duncan's feelings about the oil business went through an abrupt change. While Holt had been drilling on his property, he had received lease payments, modest but very welcome. But now that there were two producing wells on the YH—his "mother cows," he liked to call them—he received royalty payments. Now he could afford to ranch. Believing didn't occur overnight, but gradually, Duncan admitted he was a rich man.

Uncharacteristically, he decided to treat himself to three days and two nights in Fort Worth, wining and dining and throwing money around with reckless abandon. At some point during his sojourn, he ambled into an automobile dealership, and after a demonstration by a boyish, eager salesman, he found himself the owner of new Ford Model T. Two days after his return to the ranch, the car was delivered by train to the depot at Slaterton, along with the young salesman, who would teach Duncan to operate it. Mary accompanied her uncle into town for the great occasion.

By this time, Duncan was having second thoughts about the wisdom of his purchase, and he was more embarrassed than delighted by the stir the automobile's arrival caused in Slaterton. It was only the second gasoline-driven machine in the community—the first belonged to Elver Holt, who wasn't a local citizen—and the crowd that gathered around it at the depot equaled the one that had witnessed the drilling of MacGregor Number One.

Mary, naturally, fell in love with the Model T the moment she saw it. "Oh, I simply must learn to drive it!"

"Absolutely not!" Duncan roared. "Driving an automobile requires a certain mechanical ability that a woman doesn't have."

"Oh, fiddlesticks!"

"I beg your pardon, Mr. MacGregor," broke in the salesman, whose name was Adams. "We've found that women take surprisingly well to automobiling. I daresay that half the motorcars in the city have women driving them."

Duncan glared at the young man, but Mary wanted to hug him. She had started to scamper into the back seat when her uncle said, "Take the buggy home, Mary Margaret. Mr. Adams can give me my first lesson on the way back to the ranch."

Disappointed, she nevertheless did as she was told, because the buggy, after all, had to get home. But she was waiting when the car drove through the front gate. Due to Duncan's unfamiliarity with the machine, it had taken the Ford twice as long to reach the ranch as it had the buggy.

"Now then, Miss MacGregor," Mr. Adams said, beaming, "I'll show you what I've shown your uncle thus far."

Duncan looked rather shaken by his experience behind the wheel, but Mary eagerly hung on the salesman's every word.

First, he showed her how to crank the engine to get it started. Then Mary slid behind the steering wheel while Mr. Adams took the passenger's seat. "To begin, miss, you simply hook the third finger of your right hand around this throttle lever... that's right. Pull it down hard and simultaneously push your left foot on the low-speed pedal.''

The automobile responded by lurching forward with a roar. ''Now, take your foot off the pedal and ease up a mite on the throttle.'' The car catapulted into high speed with a series of jerks, and they were off. Mary threw back her head and laughed delightedly. Driving was wonderful!

MARY TOOK to driving the way she took to anything new and different—with wholehearted enthusiasm. The men, as a rule, gave the automobile a wide berth and complained noisily that it spooked the animals, but Mary behind the wheel of the Ford became a common sight around the ranch. She was forever looking for excuses to take the car into town.

''Do you need something from the general store, Hank?'' she asked one afternoon. ''I can have you there and back lickety-split.''

''I don't need a thing. If I did, I'd take a horse. You're going to kill yourself in that confounded contraption,'' Hank told her.

''No, I'm not. Promise. To prove it, I'm going to take you on a picnic Sunday, and I'll teach you to drive it.''

''Why in hell would I want to learn to drive it?''

''It's the wave of the future, Hank. Everyone will drive automobiles someday.''

"I seriously doubt that...but I'll take you up on the picnic. Are you sure you don't want to take the buggy?"

"Absolutely sure," Mary said. "That buggy is a relic of the past."

Hank eyed the Ford nervously. "How fast does this thing go?"

"The manual says if you really push it, it'll go forty miles an hour."

"Good God!"

"Don't worry. I don't think I drive nearly that fast." She frowned thoughtfully. "That's something Mr. Ford ought to do. Put a gadget in this car that will tell you how fast you're going." Executing the throttle, low-speed pedal maneuver, she and the Ford lunged forward, causing Hank to cuss and jump out of the way. Mary's laugh sounded in the still afternoon air.

SUNDAY WAS another cloudless day. Rain had become a distant memory, but for a picnic outing that was a blessing. Naturally, the Ford stirred up clouds of dust on the dirt lanes that served as roads through the ranch country. Dust was a part of driving, and Mary usually had to take a big dose of the doctor's syrup after a long drive. But she wasn't about to give up the automobile because of her affliction. She coped with the grit by covering up in a duster, hat and goggles and tying a scarf over her nose and mouth. She suggested Hank do the same.

"I'd feel like an ass," he informed her. "Just drive. I get dusty on horseback, too."

Not far from the ranch was a lake, now dried up to little more than a largish pond. But on its banks flourished dozens of stately cottonwoods, and it was beneath two of them that Mary spread a blanket and set out the contents of a wicker hamper— sandwiches, lemonade, apples and cookies.

For a time they made idle conversation while they ate. By now there existed between them an easy camaraderie that did not require constant talk. In fact, they often seemed to communicate without benefit of words at all. A nod of the head or a glance between them, and they understood each other perfectly.

And today each knew, without having discussed it with the other, that major changes in their lives loomed on the horizon. That was inevitable.

After they'd eaten, Mary carefully packed away the remains of their picnic and stashed the hamper in the car. Then she returned to sit on the blanket with Hank. She demurely took a few sips of lemonade before asking, "What are you going to do now?"

"Do?" Hank asked.

"You have some money now. I know you don't want to be a cowboy all your life."

"You're sure right about that, but I gotta tell you—hiring on at this ranch is the best thing that ever happened to me. If I hadn't, if I'd worked at a café or something until I had a big enough stake to get on to Oklahoma, I'd never have met Jimmy...or you."

Mary's eyes dipped, then came up to meet his. Hank was surprised at the solemnity he saw in them. "So...what are you going to do now?" she asked again.

"I'm not sure." He absently fingered the rim of his glass. "Looks like Holt's gonna be movin' farther west. Jimmy's been out scouting for Elver, and he thinks the pickings are better out there."

Mary took a deep breath. "Does that mean you're going with them?"

Hank had been thinking about it. Jimmy had asked him to and had spoken to Elver about him. He had a job if he wanted it. And he did. He had to learn the oil business from the ground up, but thinking about saying goodbye to Mary and never seeing her again just about flat killed him. However, better now than later. "I don't know. What about you?"

"Me?"

"You have some money, too. What are you going to do? Go back to Fort Worth? Get a job and head up some cause or the other?"

Mary smiled wanly. "I don't rightly know. Maybe."

They fell silent for a minute. Then Hank said, "You'd probably enjoy that."

"Think so?"

"Isn't it what you've always wanted?"

"I guess maybe...once." She bit her bottom lip, stared off into the distance for a few seconds, then back at him. "Hank, if you go off with the Holt crew, do you think we'll ever see each other again?"

Hank swallowed thickly. "Oh, surely we will. I can't imagine just saying goodbye and never seeing you again. Can you?"

"People change."

"Yeah, reckon they do. Why, I'll bet if I came back after a year or two, you'd be all married and probably have a young'un." He tried to laugh and couldn't.

"I don't think so," Mary said morosely. "No, I can't see that happening at all." Tossing the contents of her glass on the grass, she sighed.

Hank had never seen her in such a mood. Oh, maybe she'd been a little down in the mouth when she was expelled from the academy, but usually she was so bright and perky. He didn't know what to say. This Mary wasn't someone he knew.

They sat in silence for several minutes before Mary turned to him. "Have you had a lot of girl-friends?"

Hank didn't think about Billie Jean much any-more, and he damned sure didn't consider any of Gracie's "employees" girlfriends. He shook his head. "No."

"May I ask you a very personal question?"

"Sure."

"Do you think I'm a little bit pretty?"

He swallowed hard. "No. I think you are prob-ably the most beautiful girl in the world."

Her eyes widened. "Then I'm going to ask an-other question. Have you ever wanted to kiss me?"

Hank was so startled by the question that he couldn't find his voice for a second. Now *this* was the Mary Margaret MacGregor he knew—so bold and blunt she could take his breath away. "Only about a hundred times," he said.

Her lips curved into a slow smile. "Then why haven't you?"

"Well, shoot, Mary... I don't know. A fellow who has any sense at all doesn't grab proper ladies and kiss them."

"I'm not talking about grabbing, silly. I'm talk-ing about kissing."

"For one thing, we're not alone much."

"We're alone now. Unless you think those cows grazing over there in that pasture would be shocked."

"Mary, you are the damnedest thing I've ever met!"

"I just say what I think. You have my permission to kiss me, if you wish." Closing her eyes, she tilted her chin slightly and leaned toward him.

Hank's eyes dropped to her lips, and his heart contracted like a tight fist in his chest. Leaning forward, he closed the space between their heads and kissed her lightly, allowing his lips to remain on hers far longer than he'd meant. Then he pulled away.

Mary was as still as death, eyes still closed, breath held. Then her eyes opened, and she stared at him in wonder. "I...I guess people all over the world kiss like this every day," she said.

Hank looked at her quizzically. "Mary...that wasn't your first kiss, was it?"

She shook her head. "Just the first one I really liked."

"Oh, Lord...." He curled his hand around her nape, tucking it under her thick hair. It felt as soft as silk, and she smelled like clover. He kissed her again and felt her lean into the kiss, warmly, pliantly, and she hesitantly pressed her lips harder against his, as her hands crawled up his chest. When his arms went around her, the back of one hand accidentally brushed against the soft swell of her breast. Hank thought he was going to explode. The temptation was strong to gently guide her down on the blanket, full length against him, and...

Suddenly something in his mind snapped, and he jumped to his feet. "Lord, Mary, we've got to stop this!"

Her mouth dropped. "Stop what? Kissing?"

"Yes!"

"Why? It feels so good."

"It...leads to other things."

"Surely you don't think I would let you ravish me, I hope."

"What in hell do you know about ravishing?"

"Harriet had books, and I read them. And there's quite a lot of ravishing in the moving pictures."

Hank raked a hand through his hair. "Come on, let's go back to the ranch. If your uncle knew what we were doing, what I was *thinking,* he'd have me locked up, and they'd throw away the key. Let's go."

Mary stood and brushed at her dress. "I'm almost eighteen. My uncle cannot run my life. I know what I'm doing."

"I don't think you do."

"There's nothing wrong with kissing!" she hissed.

"No, I don't suppose there is...as long as it's nice and friendly."

"And you don't feel 'friendly' toward me?"

Hank studied her a second, his eyes dark and confused. "What I feel toward you, Mary, is so...so damned complicated that I... I don't even know how to describe it. Let's go." He scooped up the blanket, strode to the automobile and threw it in the back seat. Then he climbed into the front passenger's seat and stared glumly ahead.

Mary watched him, then sauntered to the driver's side of the car. "You're afraid of me, aren't you?" she asked as she donned the duster, hat and glasses.

"That's the dumbest thing you've ever said...and I've heard you say some pretty dumb things."

Sliding behind the steering wheel, Mary curved her finger around the throttle and gave him a knowing smile. "You are. Of course, you're not going to admit it, but you are. It's so ridiculous. I'm not in the least afraid of you, and maybe I should be. Why men like women who blush and pout and say anything but what's really on their minds is beyond me."

"Mary, you...don't understand."

"That's what I'm fond of accusing you of...not understanding, and I don't think you do half the time. But I do understand you, Hank, truly I do. So much more than you could ever imagine." The Model T lurched forward, and the ensuing roar made further conversation impossible.

MARY PURPOSELY stayed away from Hank for the next two days, just to give him plenty of time to realize how much he cared for her. She knew he did, though exactly how she knew escaped her. There was something about the way he looked at her, as if she were an ice cream soda and he wanted to eat her up. Being anything but experienced when it came to the opposite sex, she was surprised that Hank was so transparent.

And conventional. He had some nonsensical notion that she was "above" him or he was "below" her. Where had that come from? It was so much blather, the kind of thing she would have thought was reserved for snooty ladies' luncheons.

Mary was beginning to realize that getting close to a man was complicated. Hank adored her, she knew, but she was smart enough to know he was going to have to come to that conclusion himself. A few days of not seeing her would, she imagined, bring him a bit closer to that realization.

Even more surprising than knowing how he felt about her was knowing how *she* felt about *him*. She rarely thought about having a career or any of the things that had once seemed so important to her. Her mind almost always was on Hank, which amazed her. He was nothing like the heroes in Harriet's books, yet Mary knew with certainty that she wanted him with her forever. If he left, she would think about him every day of her life. Staying away from him for even two days was difficult.

She waited for him to come to the house and ask to see her, but he didn't. And since she wasn't the type to sit around waiting for things to happen, she went in search of him.

He wasn't hard to find, since most of the men were working close in that day. She spotted Hank standing near the chuck wagon, drinking coffee out of a tin cup and talking to Cookie Jenkins, the chuck boss. Nonchalantly, as if she were out for a casual afternoon stroll, she walked up to the wagon.

"Wonder if I could have a cup of your coffee, Cookie," she said. "I hear it's a mite better than what's served in the house."

Cookie chuckled. "It's a mite stronger, I'll give you that. Be glad to pour you a cup."

Hank had turned with a start at the sound of her voice.

"Good morning, Hank," she said, accepting the cup Cookie handed her.

"Good morning, Mary."

"I'd like to have a word with you, if I may."

Hank simply looked at her a minute before emptying the contents of his cup on the ground. "Sure."

They moved a few feet away from the chuck wagon. "Is there somewhere we can go that's a little more private?" Mary asked.

"Not really," he said, his eyes wandering over all the activity nearby.

"The front porch?"

"Duncan might take a damn dim view of me sittin' on the porch while everyone else is workin'."

Mary smiled knowingly. Taking a sip of coffee, she grimaced and poured it out. "Good heavens, that's terrible! How you men drink that stuff all day is beyond me. I hate coffee anyway."

"Then why did you ask for a cup?"

"Don't be obtuse. I needed an excuse to walk up to that wagon."

As usual, her candor just about floored him. "Mary, I know you didn't come out here to talk about Cookie's coffee."

"Would you like to go for a ride?"

"No!"

"Scared?"

Grabbing her arm, Hank led her around the side of a shed, partially obscuring them from the view of the others. "What do you want from me?"

Mary looked at him solemnly. "I want you to kiss me, again and again and again."

"Oh, Lord!" Hank uttered a part sigh, part groan. "You just want to be kissed. You don't care if it's me or somebody else. I just happen to be handy. I've been doing a lot of thinking lately."

"Oh, really? Well, there must be something wrong with your brain because what you've come up with is totally wrong."

"Please be sensible, though I know how hard that is for you," he said, striving for flippancy. "We'll be going our separate ways before long."

"I see. Very dramatic." She thrust the empty cup into his hand. "Well, you can fight it all you like, Hank Travis, but in case you've missed it, I'm not exactly one for letting go of something I want." She gave him an enigmatic little smile, then turned and headed back to the house.

THAT CONFRONTATION thoroughly rattled Hank. For the rest of the day he labored like a man possessed, aiming to get so tired he'd fall asleep shortly after supper that night. It worked after a fashion, though Mary was the last thing he thought of before sleep and the first the following morning. When Jed came to the bunkhouse with a long list of supplies they needed in town, Hank was the one who volunteered for the errand. He needed to get away, go someplace where he wasn't apt to run into Mary. And on the way back to the ranch he stopped to see Jimmy Blue.

"We're pulling up stakes, Hank," the geologist told him. "Are you coming or not? Gotta make up your mind."

Hank considered his options. There weren't many. The word among the oilers was that Slaterton had about played out. The wells that had been drilled in the area would continue producing for a few years, but this was no big strike. So if Hank wanted to be in the business, and he did, he would have to go elsewhere. He could go with Holt or strike out on his own, something he didn't have the resources to do...not yet.

The one thing he couldn't do was stay here, working for peon wages and eating his heart out for Mary. Someday she was going to be the mistress of a fine manor, and sure as shootin' he wasn't going to be in it with her.

"Count me in," he said, wondering how it was possible to feel so absolutely wretched when he was being offered what he'd always wanted. "When are you leaving?"

"Right away," Jimmy said. "If you can check in by, say, next Wednesday, that'll be fine. You realize you're going to be nothing but a green boll weevil."

"I know, but I gotta start somewhere. I'll be there."

Hank rode out of the Holt camp and raced like the wind back to the ranch. He had to tell Duncan immediately. That was a courtesy. Cowboys were a notoriously itchy-footed bunch who picked up and left whenever the mood struck. But Duncan had been mighty good to him; he owed the man a week's notice.

There was an outside door to Duncan's office, one the ranch hands were free to use at will. It spared them having to clomp through the front of the elegant house. Hank tethered his horse, knocked on the door and waited for the rancher's summons. Then he stepped into the office.

Duncan looked up from his desk. "Ah, Hank. What can I do for you?"

Hank removed his hat and stood nervously before the desk. Funny, but he was going to miss this man. He didn't miss the peanut farm in South Texas, but he was going to miss Duncan MacGregor. As for Mary, he wouldn't let himself even think about her.

"Duncan... I have something to tell you. Elver Holt has offered me a job, and...well, I reckon I'm gonna take it. I guess I'll be leaving next week."

Duncan sat back in his chair and folded his arms across his belly. "Hate to see you go, Hank. You've made us a good hand."

"Thanks. I want to tell you that I can't imagine a better man to work for than you, sir."

"Does Mary know about this?" Duncan asked quietly.

"No."

"You're friends, aren't you?"

"Yes."

"Don't you think you oughta tell her?"

"Yes, sir, and I will, but I thought I should tell you first."

"I see. Well, I won't say anything to her. I'll leave that to you." The rancher heaved himself out of his chair and stuck out his hand, which Hank took. "Best of luck to you, son. If you're ever back this way, stop in to see me."

"Thank you, Duncan. I'll be talkin' to you."

Hank stepped back and turned to leave, but at that minute the door that led to the main part of the house opened and Mary entered the office. "Duncan, I—" She stopped. "Oh, Hank."

"Hank stopped by to tell you something, Mary Margaret."

"Oh?" Mary looked at Hank. "What is it?"

He'd never felt more awkward in his life. She looked so pretty, all dressed in yellow again, that she made his heart ache, and he wondered where he was going to find the words to say what had to be said.

"Well, Mary, I ... Could we go outside or something?"

"Of course. This way." She led him through the house and out the door onto the front porch. There she turned. "Well?"

"Could we . . . sit down?"

Mary eyed him warily but said nothing, merely crossed the veranda and sat on the porch swing. Hank stood in front of her, fingering the hat in his hand. "Now . . . what did you want to tell me?"

"There's no easy way to say this. I'm leaving."

Hank noticed the working of her throat as she swallowed hard a couple of times. And he didn't think he imagined the trembling of her chin. "When?" she asked.

"Next week."

"Isn't that sudden?"

"Not really."

Mary folded her hands in her lap and stared at them a minute. "So, you made up your mind."

"Yes." In a sudden move, Hank closed the space between them and sat down beside her. "I'd feel so much better if I knew what you were going to do."

She turned, and he was startled to see tears in her eyes. "What possible difference can it make to you what I do now?"

"It just . . . does. Will you get a job? You're not going to stay here at the ranch, are you?"

"Heaven forbid."

"Then . . . what?"

A minute or two of strained silence followed. Then Mary's chin came up defiantly, and Hank saw the look on her face he had seen so many times before—stubborn, immovable. "You haven't left me much choice. I'm going to go with you."

Hank couldn't have been more surprised if she'd kicked him. "What?"

"You heard me."

"Mary... you can't!"

"Why not?"

Hank had to remember that Mary wasn't a woman easily reasoned with. In fact, it was impossible to reason with her because she didn't think like most women. "There must be a hundred good reasons why you can't come to the oil fields with me."

"Then give me one."

"Well, I... For one thing, oilers work out in the boondocks most of the time. They work long hours, and the work's dirty. More than dirty. It's filthy. There's no room for women in that kind of atmosphere."

"Oh, pooh! Are you going to tell me that no one in the oil business is married?"

Hank's eyes widened. *"Married?"*

"Of course, *married*. What in heaven's name did you think I was suggesting?" She nonchalantly smoothed at her dress, as casually as if she had just suggested having lemonade. "I'd be very unhappy without you, Hank, and whether you realize it or not, you'd be unhappy without me, too. So if you're determined to work in the oil fields, you're just going to have to marry me and take me with you. Otherwise, I'll follow you and cause all sorts of scandal.''

She had left him astonished on more occasions than he could remember, but now he was thunderstruck. "Mary, I . . . I can't marry you. I'm a farm kid. I've been a cowpoke. All the money I have in the world is the little bit I made off those wells. Now I'm going to be a roughneck, at the very bottom of the ladder. I may never have a lot of money, and you . . . well, you belong in a house like this.''

"How tiresome! I would expire from boredom within a year." Placing a hand on his shirtsleeve, she gave him her sweetest smile. "Tell me the truth . . . down deep in your heart, wouldn't you like to be married to me?''

"Oh, Mary. . . ." Hank's shoulders rose and fell, and he rubbed his forehead. "You're the damnedest thing! I'd make the world's worst husband.''

"Well, come to think of it, I wouldn't make such a terrific wife, either, so maybe we ought to stick together and spare other people from having to put up with us.''

He shook his head. "This is just another adventure for you, don't you see?''

"No, I don't." She was silent a minute, then declared, "You don't want me. Is that what you're having such a hard time saying? You're leaving because it's the easiest way to get me out of your life.''

Hank was horrified. "Oh, Mary, *no!* You can't ever think that. I think... well, I think I'm gonna miss you every day of my life."

"Then what is it? Why are you hemming and hawing about marrying me?"

"I... I refuse to be responsible for ruining your chances for a grand future." He sounded pompous even to himself.

"Future? What kind of future do you think I'd have here?"

"But the city... a career. You have money now and you'll be eighteen soon. You can do anything you choose."

"Fine. I choose to go with you."

Hank didn't understand his own emotions. Why wasn't he whooping for joy? She was trying to give him everything he'd ever wanted. "Are you really serious about this, Mary?"

"Very. So answer my question. Would you like to be married to me?"

Hank gave up. "Of course I would."

"And you do love me, don't you?"

"Of course I do."

"And I love you."

"You deserve so much more. The moon and the stars."

"What on earth would I do with the moon and stars? I *want* you."

Hank took a couple of deep breaths. "Then I guess you've got me."

Mary laughed delightedly, threw her arms around his neck and kissed him soundly. When she pulled away, she looked at him with eyes sparkling like diamonds. "Let's go tell Duncan."

"Mary, I really think you ought to think about this for a few days."

"You didn't give me a few days to think about it. There must be a hundred things we have to do before next week."

Hopping to her feet, she ran to the door, and a bemused Hank, staggered by this newest twist of fate, followed her.

CHAPTER FIVE

DUNCAN'S FACE TURNED the color of a Hereford's hide when he heard the announcement. *"What?"* he thundered. "You're out of your minds!"

Hank could feel himself almost quaking in his boots, but Mary looked completely calm and unruffled. "We've thought about this, Duncan, and it's what we want to do," she said in that crisp way of hers.

"Oh, really? Well, let me tell you, young lady, you're far too young to get married."

"Mama married at seventeen. I'm almost eighteen."

Duncan focused his attention on Hank. "And how old are you?"

"I'll be twenty in December, sir."

"Twenty. A lad! A mere pup!" The rancher glared at his niece. "So...you want to go off to the back of beyond with this kid, do you? To live in a shack? To move every year to another depressing boom town? To have a passel of babies you can't feed?"

"Now, beggin' your pardon, Duncan," Hank said, unable to keep quiet. "That's not the life I'm going to give Mary."

"Oh, no? Are you going to give her all this?" Duncan's hand made a sweep to indicate the YH Ranch as a whole.

"Not right away, of course, but—"

"Well, let me tell you something about this girl you want for a wife. She can't cook. She can't sew. She's never had to clean a house—"

"I used to clean house when I was in Crystal Creek! I had to clean my room at the academy," Mary protested.

Duncan ignored her. "She can't do one damned thing that would make her a decent wife. Put it out of your minds. It's not going to happen." He met Mary's icy stare. "Wait until your mama hears about this. Go to your room."

Mary was furious. "I'm no longer a child who can be sent to her room at an adult's convenience! Hank, do something!"

Hank stepped closer to her and laid a hand on her arm. "Mary... honey, this isn't doing anyone any good. Please, just wait outside, and I'll talk to you in a bit."

She hesitated, glaring at her uncle for a minute. Then, with a swish of her skirts, she stormed out of the room. The two men stared at each other in silence until Duncan finally spoke.

"Somehow I don't believe you conspired behind my back, son."

"No, sir, I didn't."

"Then am I to assume all this was Mary Margaret's idea?"

"No, sir, not entirely. I'm not sure I would have found the nerve to bring up the subject in the first place, but the point is . . . I love her very much. I'd be honored to have her as my wife."

Duncan snorted. "What is 'love' at nineteen is often something entirely different at thirty. Tell you what I'm gonna do. Only the biggest favor anyone's ever done you. I'm going to send two of the men to escort you to the depot in town. Get your belongings and draw your pay. I'd like you on your way before the day's over."

"Duncan, I can't do that to Mary!"

"Listen, Hank, that girl would drive you ragged before a year was out. You'd be beggin' me to take her back. Count your blessings. Someday you'll thank me."

Hank was impotent with rage . . . and worry. There was no question that Duncan could indeed ride him out of town on a rail if he so chose. For one thing, one of the rancher's best friends was the sheriff, and the sheriff was a law unto himself in these parts. "Duncan, I'll leave . . . but please let me talk to Mary first."

Duncan seemed to consider that a minute, but then he shook his head. "Nope. Don't think so. Won't serve any useful purpose. She'll cry and sulk for a few days, but she'll get over it and so will you."

Hank summoned every last ounce of bravado he could muster. "What...what if I refuse to go?"

A slow smile crossed Duncan's face. "You can't refuse. You've been fired and ordered to leave. The boys who take you into town will have...er, persuaders."

Hank's shoulders sagged. It wasn't fair, it was wrong, but there it was. By the time Mary realized he was gone, he'd be just that—gone. He realized he'd never even told her the name of the place where Holt was setting up a new camp, not that her knowing would do them any good.

And he took the time to wonder if he had ever actually thought, for even a minute, that he really was going to marry Mary Margaret MacGregor.

"Hank," Duncan said solemnly, "I'm not doing this because I don't like you. I think you're a fine young fellow. But you and my niece don't belong together. All I'm doing is saving both of you from making a terrible mistake."

Feeling more helpless than he ever had in his life, Hank turned on his heel and left the office. Maybe when enough time had passed that he could look at this realistically, he would come to agree with

Duncan. Mary deserved everything, and he had nothing to offer her. Maybe marrying Mary *was* the worst thing he could do to her.

IN THE HALL outside the office, Mary paced restlessly, her mind spinning. Occasionally she would stop and press her ear against the door, but all she heard was the muted sound of voices. She had no idea what they were saying. Then she would resume her pacing.

For what seemed like an hour but could only have been fifteen minutes or so, she waited for something to happen. She was good and worried. Hank had a great deal of respect for authority, and Duncan could be the most authoritarian man imaginable. Would Hank put up a real fight?

Another fifteen minutes or so passed. Then the door to the office opened, and Duncan stepped out into the hall. Seeing his niece, he frowned. "I thought you were supposed to be in your room."

Mary ignored that. "Where's Hank?"

"Gone."

"Gone? What do you mean *gone?*"

"He came to his senses and decided I was right." Duncan tried to step around her with no success.

"I don't believe that," Mary said. "Where is he?"

"He has left the ranch. Let it be, Mary Margaret."

"I won't let it be!" she all but screamed. "I'll never forgive you for this, Duncan. Never!" Turning, she fled up the stairs.

Heaving a weary sigh, Duncan went into the parlor. What he needed was a stiff shot of whiskey. Fortunately, he thought, affairs of the heart at eighteen were not usually fatal. His niece would get over this and get on with her life.

Duncan had not yet learned not to underestimate the determination of Mary Margaret Mac-Gregor.

THE DEPOT IN SLATERTON was hot and smelled of stale tobacco. Hank added to the problem by smoking cigarette after cigarette and pacing the floor. The two YH cowhands who had "accompanied" him to town were indeed packing pistols. Hank wondered if they'd actually use them—not that he intended finding out.

One of them was new at the YH; Hank barely knew him. But the other man was a fellow named Ernest, who'd been at the ranch almost as long as Hank. While they weren't exactly friends, they had spent some time together, and Hank was banking on Ernest's trust.

"Let's step outside for a minute, Ernest. The air in here is foul, and there's something I want to ask you."

The cowpoke glanced around uncertainly, then shrugged. "Why not?" he said, getting to his feet.

Outside the depot, the dust-choked air wasn't much better, but there was no one around to hear the men's conversation.

"I want you to do a favor for me, Ernest," Hank said. "It's pretty important."

"Well, sure, if I can. What in hell did you do to get MacGregor steamed at you?"

"I wanted to marry his niece."

Ernest whistled. "Maybe I'd better stay out of this."

"All I want you to do is give Mary a note from me."

"How in hell am I going to get close enough to her to give her a note?"

"Figure out a way. I know...put it in the scat of that car. She's the only one who ever drives it. She'll find it. I just can't leave without saying goodbye."

Ernest pondered this a minute. "Ever' speck of good sense I have tells me to stay out of this."

"*Please.*"

A couple of seconds of silence passed. Then Ernest said, "Aw, hell . . . all right."

Relieved, Hank reached in his pocket for the little stub of a pencil he usually carried. Then it occurred to him that he didn't have any paper. Glancing around, he saw a dozen or so public notices tacked to the depot wall. He tore one off, turned it over, braced it against the wall and began to write.

But he'd gotten no farther than *Dear Mary, I want you to know that...* when there was some sort of commotion in the street. He looked toward the sound, blinked and looked again. There, stirring up a miniature cyclone, spooking chickens and causing tethered horses to stomp and snort, was Mary in the Model T.

"Reckon you ain't gonna need that note, Hank," Ernest said with a grin. "Tell the lady herself what you want her to know."

Hank watched in disbelief as the car came to a shuddering halt at the depot steps. Mary got out, reached into the back seat and pulled out a valise. She was having some difficulty carrying it, so Hank hopped down and took it out of her hand. The thing must have weighed fifty pounds.

"Mary! What are you doing?"

"I'm taking a trip. Would you be so kind as to take my bag in to the ticket agent?"

"Where in the hell are you going?"

She turned and looked him in the eyes. Hers were full of fire and brimstone, and the set to her mouth seemed carved in granite. "Wherever you are," she said crisply.

Hank stepped closer to her and lowered his voice. "You are going to get me shot!"

"Fiddlesticks. Duncan's not going to shoot anybody."

Ernest stepped forward. "Beggin' your pardon, ma'am, but my orders are to put Hank on the next westbound train and—"

"Fine," Mary said. "Then you'll be following orders exactly, won't you? Will one of you kindly take my bag inside?"

Hank set the bag on the steps, then placed his hands on her upper arms. "Mary...honey...you can't do this. Listen, I was just writing a note for Ernest here to give to you. I've been thinking. I'll go on to the camp, and in a couple of months I'll come back for you. While I'm gone I'll write you all the time. When Duncan sees how determined we are—"

"Unacceptable, Hank. I'm going with you."

"Please be reasonable. You can't just pack up and leave like that."

"You did," she said, skewering him with the stubbornness in her dark eyes. "I could hardly believe it when Duncan told me you were gone."

"That's different. I was threatened. Besides, I'm nothing but a cowhand, who can roam at will. You're a lady, and you have obligations."

"Such as?"

Hank heaved a heavy sigh. "Well, for instance, what are you going to do about that blasted automobile?"

"I'll ask the ticket agent to have someone take it back to the ranch."

"No one else in town can drive the damned thing."

Mary glanced at the car, then back at Hank. "Then it can stay here till Judgment Day as far as I'm concerned. Now, I have to go inside and purchase my ticket to...to wherever. Where *are* we going, by the way?"

"*I'm* going to a place called Prairie Gap."

Mary blanched, swallowed hard and smiled. "Sounds lovely. I'm sure I'll enjoy it tremendously."

"I don't have the slightest idea what it's like. The living conditions might be terrible."

"I'll survive, Hank. I'm going."

All of a sudden there was another racket in the street, and Hank looked over Mary's shoulder to see Duncan and two more YH cowboys riding like the wind, bearing down on them.

"Oh-oh," Ernest said and disappeared into the depot.

"Hold on! Hold on! Don't anybody move! Get out of my way!" Duncan shouted over the sound of the horses' hooves. Reining in, he slid out of the saddle and hustled over to stand in front of Hank and Mary, arms akimbo. "What in the devil do you think you're doing, young lady?"

"I'm going with Hank."

"I figured as much. Yeah, when I saw that automobile sailing through the gate, I pretty well figured what you were up to. If you aren't the
goddangedest..." Duncan's chest heaved. He made
fists of his hands, and Hank wondered if he intended using them. Damned if he wanted to get in
a fight with a man Duncan's age.

But suddenly, like air oozing out of a balloon, the
defiance left Duncan. He fastened a stony expression on his niece. "No, you're not. You're not getting on a train with a fellow and going off to God
knows where without being married to him."

Hank and Mary exchanged startled expressions.
"Oh, Duncan," Mary gasped, "do you mean..."

"Your mama would whomp the livin' daylights
out of me if I let you go off and get hitched by a
justice of the peace in some backwater. The least we
can do for her is get Preacher Rollins to do it all
properlike. Now climb in that damned automobile
and go back to the ranch... both of you."

Mary let out a very unladylike whoop, threw her
arms around her uncle's waist and hugged him ferociously. "Oh, thank you, thank you."

Hank wondered how many more surprises the
day had in store for him. He stuck out his hand.
"Thanks, sir. Thanks a lot."

Mary gleefully ran for the automobile, while
Duncan pumped Hank's hand. "Son, since the day
that girl entered my life, it's just been one god-

damn thing after another. What you're fixin' to get hitched up with . . . well, I wouldn't wish it on a snake.''

NO LONGER a YH cowhand and now engaged to the owner's niece, Hank found his station in life had dramatically improved. He was given the attic guest room, a charmingly appointed private haven, certainly a dozen or so notches above anything he had stayed in before. He ate three wonderful meals a day in the big house's dining room and was already treated like a member of the family. Best of all, as an engaged couple, he and Mary were left alone to do pretty much as they pleased. Hank was living an idyll.

But three nights before the wedding, as he lay in the guest room's comfortable bed contemplating the ceiling, he was seized by a spasm of fear. All of this had happened awfully fast, and he wondered if he was ready for it. Could he take care of a wife? Could he reconcile the life he had chosen—one of men and machines, sweat and profanity—with the life he thought Mary should have? He stared at the ceiling and no answers came.

Damn, where were those visions of his when he really needed them? He was only twenty and had little concept of the word *marriage*. He tried to envision being a parent, and nothing at all came to him. Thinking back to his own mother and father, all he could remember was a lot of hard work. Not once had he seen them laugh and hug and joke. He couldn't bear thinking that marriage would do that to Mary and himself.

At that moment the door to his room opened. Raising himself up on his elbows, he saw Mary silhouetted in the doorway. "Mary?" he exclaimed.

"You weren't asleep, were you?" she whispered.

"No."

"May I come in?"

"Well, I ... I'm sure Duncan wouldn't like this a bit."

Mary closed the door softly behind her and silently crossed the room. She was wearing a robe, and her feet were bare. She squatted on the floor beside the bed, placed a hand on his arm and smiled. "What difference does it make? I'll be your wife in three days and can come into your room any time I please, since it will be my room, too. Nice thought, isn't it?" Leaning over him, she kissed him soundly on the mouth.

Hank studied her—took in her freshly scrubbed face, her shining hair—and was painfully aware that between her and his totally naked body was a sheet, nothing else. He shifted to one side, hoping that would keep his instant arousal from becoming too evident.

"Mary, honey...you probably should go to your own room."

"I will in a minute. I came up here to ask you something. Are you having second thoughts... about us, about marriage?"

Lord, sometimes he thought she could read his mind. "No," he fibbed.

"I'd think it was awfully strange if you didn't," Mary said solemnly. "Men are supposed to fight it so. But I came up here to tell you that you don't have a thing to worry about."

"I don't?"

She shook her head. "No, nothing. Because no matter where you go or what you decide to do, I'm going to be there. And you'll find out it's much easier to do anything with someone who loves you than by yourself."

"How come you know so much about marriage?"

"I just feel it... right here." She took his hand and pressed it just below her left breast. A choking sound came from deep in Hank's throat. "You'll always be you, and I'll always be me, and we're going to get along just fine."

She amazed him, as always. Not only was she a daredevil and a gambler, she was an optimist. How could the world ever drag down someone like Mary? "If you say so, I'm sure that's the way it's going to be."

Mary dropped his hand and placed hers on his chest, right over his heart. "I'm very, very excited about all this."

Hank laced his fingers through her dark hair, then curled a long tendril around his forefinger. He wished he could say something eloquent and memorable, but nothing came to him. He felt as tongue-tied as he'd been at sixteen when in the presence of a pretty girl. He experienced a great rush of protectiveness toward her, which was a mite ridiculous. Mary needed less protecting than anyone he knew. "I'm excited, too, honey, but right now...I really think you ought to go to your own room. Having you here is...well, it's difficult for me."

"All right, but first..." She leaned over and kissed him again, her baby-soft lips tantalizing in their eagerness. Straightening, she said, "I'll see you at breakfast."

Hank watched her leave, then willed his body back to normalcy. He wasn't going to worry anymore. Together, he and Mary were going to do just fine.

IT WAS A QUIET, lovely wedding, though hastily arranged. They'd had less than a week to put it together, but Mary wouldn't have changed a minute of it. A dozen of Duncan's friends, along with most of the YH's hired hands, made up the guest list. Mary wore her only white dress and Hank his only suit. A neighboring rancher's wife had fashioned a bouquet from her garden.

Emma and Mary's brothers were also in attendance, though with some reluctance. When Duncan had wired his sister-in-law with news about the wedding, Emma had boarded the first train north and arrived at the YH full of alarm, wondering aloud if her daughter had lost her mind. There had been some tense, awkward moments when Duncan had felt rather sorry for Hank. It couldn't have been easy for him, knowing Emma didn't consider him a suitable husband for Mary.

But there never had been any real doubt about the outcome. Mary wanted Hank, so Mary would have Hank, and the rest of the world could get used to it.

After cake and punch were served, Mary disappeared upstairs to change into her traveling suit while Hank gathered their luggage and put it on the front veranda. He stood around shaking hands and accepting the good wishes of the men he had worked with for so long. Then the bride put in an appearance, dressed in a rose-colored suit with leg-of-mutton sleeves. Mary staunchly refused to wear a corset, so unlike the other women present, she looked soft and utterly feminine in her clothes, not stiff and uncomfortable. Hank thought she was the most beautiful person in the world, and couldn't get used to the idea that she was his wife.

Jed was going to drive the newlyweds to the depot in a buggy, but Duncan had one last surprise for them.

"Take that confounded thing," he said, pointing to the Model T.

Mary's mouth dropped, and one hand flew to her chest. "Oh, Duncan...do you mean it?"

"Of course I do," her uncle said gruffly. "What in hell would I do with the contraption? Consider it my wedding present to you."

Mary screeched with delight, but Hank wasn't sure how he felt about ownership of an automobile. It seemed to him to be more of a nuisance than anything, but Mary was clearly overjoyed by the gift. He didn't think he wanted to start married life by denying his bride something she obviously coveted. And that minute he made up his mind to learn to drive the ridiculous thing. It would be downright embarrassing to have to depend on his wife for his transportation.

The luggage was loaded into the car instead of the buggy, and amid a flurry of hugs, handshakes and goodbyes, Hank and Mary drove away from the YH. Several miles down the road, she let the Ford come to a halt.

"Where are we going?" she asked.

"Lord, Mary, I'm not sure." Why hadn't he given any thought to where they would spend their wedding night?

"I don't think we can make it very far before sunset, and I've never driven at night."

Hank had been afraid of this; the car was a problem. Without it, they could have simply boarded a train. It was on the tip of his tongue to suggest that they take the blasted automobile back to the ranch and get Jed to drive them to the depot, where they could catch the train as planned. But instinct told him what his darling Mary would have thought of that idea.

"Maybe the boardinghouse in Slaterton," Mary suggested. "Mrs. Harding might have a vacancy just for one night."

Hank could have kicked himself. Forcing his bride to spend her wedding night in a boardinghouse was unforgivable, but there wasn't much he could do about it at this point. "It's worth a try," he said lamely.

Loretta Harding, the boardinghouse proprietress, was a large, expansive woman. Until the arrival of the oilers she had been the motherly sort, always willing to throw open her doors to anyone in need of a room. Now she had developed a suspicious attitude toward new boarders, but the young couple standing on the porch, all dressed in their finery, aroused no suspicion.

"Good afternoon," she greeted them. "What can I do for you?"

"Hello, Mrs. Harding," Mary said politely. "Do you remember me?"

"Duncan MacGregor's niece, right? Mary, isn't it?"

"Yes, ma'am, and this is Hank Travis, my husband. We were married this afternoon."

Lucille beamed. "How nice! You're a lucky man, Mr. Travis."

"Thank you, ma'am. I think so."

"Mrs. Harding," Mary said, "we seem to have a problem. We're traveling west, but we have an automobile, and I don't know how to drive after dark. We were wondering if you have a room we could rent . . . just for one night."

Lucille's face fell. "Oh, dear me, I'm so sorry, but I'm plain full up. An hour or so ago I could've let you have the two cots on the sleeping porch, but I rented them to two salesmen. 'Least, that's what they say they are. I plan to keep an eye on 'em, I'll tell you."

The woman apologized profusely, but the fact remained—there was no room. Dejectedly, Hank and Mary returned to the car and pondered their problem. "I'm beginning to think that the only solution to this," Hank said, "is to go back to the ranch. You can get a good night's sleep in your room, and I'll sleep in the bunkhouse. Tomorrow we'll get an early start."

Mary was horrified. "How humiliating, Hank! To admit right off the bat that we can't take care of our problems."

"Mary, be reasonable."

"No! We'll think of something." She rubbed her stomach. "But right now, could we find something to eat? I was too excited all day to do anything but nibble, and now I'm starved."

"Well . . . there's always Barney's."

"Then Barney's it is."

EVERY HEAD in the café turned when Hank and Mary entered. The eatery was a clean, respectable establishment, but its clientele was mostly cowboys and roughnecks, with a few local merchants thrown in, and no one bothered to dress up to eat there. Hank and Mary self-consciously made their way to a table in the rear and studied the menu on the chalkboard behind the counter.

"Have you ever eaten here?" she asked.

"Plenty of times."

"What should I order?"

"The stew's not too bad."

Mary nodded uncertainly. "Splendid. I'll have the stew."

Barney himself, his ample girth encased in a soiled apron, took their order. "Howdy, Hank. You folks been to a funeral?"

"No, Barney. As a matter of fact, we got married this afternoon. This is my wife, Mary."

Barney looked astonished. "You don't say! Well, congratulations. So you're havin' your wedding dinner at my place, huh?"

"Not meaning to be disrespectful, Barney, but we didn't have a hell of a lot of choice," Hank said, smiling.

Barney laughed. "Yeah, I don't have much competition, that's for sure. It's either me, the boardinghouse or one of those dives like Gracie's. What'll you have?"

"My wife would like a bowl of your famous stew. 'Spose you could scoop off a spoonful or two of grease?"

"I'll try. How 'bout you, Hank?"

"The same."

"You don't want any grease, either?"

"Please, no." Hank wished with all his heart that he'd given tonight some thought. He looked across the table at Mary. The word *beautiful* didn't do her justice. For all her feistiness, she could look very prim and proper and ladylike when the mood struck, and that was the way she looked now. Tonight she should have been at some fancy restaurant in Fort Worth, maybe at a place the Swifts and Armours patronized, complete with linens and candles and...well, he wasn't sure what all, but certainly more than a bare table at Barney's Café.

The stew was a little better than usual, possibly due to the absence of so much grease. Hank and Mary made idle conversation, as though they were on a date instead of fresh from their wedding vows, but Hank knew she had to be concerned about where they would spend the night. His mind spun. There was no place in the miserable town that had rooms...unless...

He'd never know why the idea occurred to him. He dismissed it over and over, but it came back, more insistently each time. It was ludicrous, of course, but it was the only thing he could think of. Did he dare?

When they'd finished their stew, Barney brought coffee to them. "Got dried-apple pie," he announced proudly. "Made 'em fresh this morning. A piece would go awful good with a cup of coffee."

Mary pressed a napkin to her lips. "Oh, I don't really think..."

Hank quickly reached across the table and took one of her hands. "Mary, I just remembered something I've gotta do. It won't take but a couple of minutes. Why don't you have your coffee and a piece of pie, and I'll be right back."

"Right back? But where are you going?"

"Just to...take care of a matter. Really, by the time you finish your pie, I'll be back."

Mary thought a second, then shrugged. "Well, all right." She looked up at Barney. "I'll have the pie, thank you."

Hank patted her hand and jumped to his feet. "I'll be right back, promise," he said as he hurried out of the café.

Outside, he turned right and ran as fast as he could. In a minute or less he burst through the door of Gracie's.

It was too early for there to be much of a crowd. A waitress behind the front counter eyed him curiously. "Where's Gracie?" Hank asked.

She gave a jerk of her head. "Back there, in her office."

"Thanks," he said and hurried off, oblivious to the stares of the joint's few customers. The door to the office was slightly ajar, and he could see Gracie seated at the desk, writing something. He stepped inside and cleared his throat.

Gracie looked up, and her face broke into a smile of welcome. She was a full-figured woman with silver hair, who dressed flamboyantly, usually in red, but expensively, and the diamonds on her lobes, at her neck and on her fingers attested to her success as a "businesswoman." Earlier, when Hank still followed the crowd to her establishment on Saturday nights, she had taken a liking to the young cowhand, whom she considered a gentleman and a cut above her usual regulars. "Why, Hank honey,

I haven't seen you in a month of Sundays. My, don't you look nice! Goin' to a party?"

"No, Gracie, as a matter of fact, I got married this afternoon."

"You don't say! Well, congratulations." She frowned. "Then what in hell are you doing here?"

"I've got a real problem. Y'see . . . my wife and I don't have any place to stay tonight. We're heading west, but it's gonna be dark before long, and she has this automobile, and . . . Well, we need a place to stay awful bad. The boardinghouse is full, and I . . . I was wondering if you could help me out."

"You want to bring your wife *here?*"

Hank swallowed hard, barely believing he was doing this. "I tell you . . . I'm pretty desperate."

"You must be."

"I told her we ought'a go back to the YH, but she won't hear of it."

"The YH?" Gracie peered at him thoughtfully. "Is your wife by any chance Duncan MacGregor's niece?"

"Yes, that's Mary." Hank didn't want to ponder too heavily on just how it was that Gracie knew Duncan.

"Pretty little dark-haired thing? A real lady, right?"

"Right."

Gracie drummed her long red fingernails on the desktop for a few seconds, then stood. "Come here, Hank. I want to show you something."

The other door to the office opened onto the alley in back. Hank followed Gracie outside, his eyes tracking the direction of her gesturing finger. "That stairway there leads to my private rooms, and they're just as nice as can be," she said. "That's the only entrance. You and your little bride can stay up there. I'll bunk with one of the girls."

"Gracie, you sweetheart! How can I ever thank you?"

"Don't bother. I'm doing it for Duncan as much as for you." She winked at him. "Can't have that niece of his sleeping just anywhere."

An alarming thought crossed Hank's mind. "Gracie, you won't ever let Duncan know where we spent our wedding night, will you?"

"Oh, he'd probably get a big laugh out of it."

Hank looked pained. "Believe me, Duncan doesn't have much of a sense of humor when it comes to Mary."

Gracie chuckled. "Okay, he'll never know. By the way, where is she?"

"Oh, I left her having pie and coffee at Barney's."

"Well, go get her. Just give me a few minutes to get some things, then bring her here. Park that automobile back here, and no one will bother it. But the two of you best clear out before this joint starts to stir around noon.''

"Oh, we'll be gone long before that. Gracie, you can't imagine what you've done for me. I was just sick thinking that maybe Mary and I were going to have to sleep in the car tonight. Let me pay you.''

She laughed lustily. "You don't have enough money. Now don't let your bride cool her heels any longer. Go get her, and I'll make sure my rooms are ready for a lady. Get now.''

Again Hank stammered his thanks, then turned and trotted toward Barney's.

CHAPTER SIX

MARY PULLED the Model T into the spot Hank indicated, then looked around. "What is this place, Hank?"

"It belongs to a sorta friend of mine. She said we could have it for the night."

"She? A girl?"

"A woman. Actually, she's old enough to be my grandma."

"So how come you know her?"

Hank sighed. "Mary, honey, don't ask so many questions. We have a room for the night. Be thankful. It's right up at the top of those stairs. You go on up, and I'll bring your suitcase. Which one you want?"

"The smaller one. Aren't you bringing yours up?"

"Don't reckon I'll be needing much in the way of clothes tonight." Turning to the task, he didn't see the blush that pinkened Mary's cheeks before she turned and went up the stairs.

"Oh, Hank!" she exclaimed when he joined her. "Your friend must be terribly rich. Look at all these lovely things."

The parlor was a study in Victorian splendor, full of velvet, fringe and patterns of every description. "I suppose Gracie does all right," he said.

"What does she do?" Mary asked, her eyes roaming around the room.

"She's in business."

"What kind of business?"

"She . . . er, owns the bar downstairs."

"A bar?"

"Yes, a bar. I'll put your bag in the bedroom."

Mary followed him and stood in the doorway while he set her bag on the floor at the foot of the bed. The bed was enormous, twice as big as the one in her room at the ranch. It had a thick quilted spread, and she also noticed lace curtains at the windows. "Hard to believe a lady who owns all these lovely things would also own a bar."

"Somebody's got to own them." Straightening, Hank appraised her, and with his fingertip he traced the outline of her mouth. "I've been dying to kiss you all day."

"You did, remember? When the preacher said, 'You may kiss the bride,' I seem to recall you did."

"That little peck wasn't a kiss. *This* is a kiss."

Mary's heart fluttered when he joined his lips to hers. They hadn't kissed more than two dozen times, and they'd never kissed like this. It was slow and languorous, deliciously sweet and prolonged. When the tip of his tongue pierced the seam of her lips, forcing them apart, she felt as though a bolt of lightning had struck her. And she realized that nothing in Harriet's books had prepared her for a real kiss. She didn't ever want it to end. Locking her hands behind his neck, she held his head tightly against hers, and the kiss deepened. They kissed until they were breathless and had to break apart.

"My goodness!" Mary said, breathing hard.

Hank chuckled. "You liked it?"

"Oh, my, yes!"

"And you're not afraid of me?"

Her eyes opened wide. "Afraid of you? Oh, no, Hank, not at all. I could never be afraid of you. Besides being my husband, you're my best friend."

"And you're not afraid of tonight...the thing that comes next?"

She shook her head. "I don't think so. You mean the marriage bed, don't you? No, I don't think so."

He fingered one of the buttons of her suit jacket. "What's underneath this?"

"A chemise."

"What's that?"

She smiled at him lazily. "See for yourself."

Hank flicked the buttons from their holes and pushed the jacket off her shoulders, then let it fall to the floor. The thing called a chemise was a wisp of a garment with straps. It bared her shoulders, her arms and a good part of her chest. A strip of lace covered the area where her breasts began swelling. Her skin looked like ivory. His heart began thumping like mad. "I've... I've never seen your arms before," he said in awe.

"Well, I should hope not!" she exclaimed in mock horror. "What would a lady be doing showing her bare arms to a man?"

"Your skin...." He placed his hands on both her shoulders, then let them drift down her arms. "It's so smooth. I don't think I've ever felt anything so smooth before." His hands roamed up again, and his fingers laced through her hair. "You must have the most beautiful hair in the world."

"Oh, me," Mary said with a catch in her voice. "You're giving me goose bumps. Why... why haven't you even taken off your coat and tie?"

"You want me undressed, huh? Good idea." He shrugged out of his coat, and it joined Mary's jacket on the floor. Ripping off the string tie that had threatened to choke him all day, he undid the buttons of his starched white shirt and jerked it free of his trousers. Bracing his arms on the wall on either side of her head, he asked, "Is that better?"

Mary's eyes were fastened on his hard, brown, hairless chest. With her fingertips she stroked it. "Oh, Hank, your chest is so...smooth. As smooth as my arms, I'll bet."

"I still can't believe you're mine."

"I've been yours a long time, long before tonight. Maybe since the first time I talked to you at the corral."

"That seems so long ago. Back then, I wasn't even supposed to *talk* to you."

"Well, you can do lots more than 'talk' to me now. There was a line in those books of Harriet's ... I'll swear it was in every single one of them. It went, 'I'm yours to do with as you wish.' I really am. Really."

Hank was having a damnably difficult time taking this slow and easy, but there was a lot at stake. He had heard stories of brides who cried for hours on their wedding night, and he didn't want that to happen to Mary. Just how all this turned out was up to him, and that was scary. He wasn't a man with vast experience with women, and his previous sexual encounters had not required finesse, so he supposed he and Mary were going to learn a lot together.

He bent his head to kiss her, and this time he found eager, parted lips and arms that wound around him like snakes. As he deepened the kiss, he felt her body sway. He, too, was having a hard time staying on his feet, so, without breaking the kiss, he gently guided her to the bed, pushed her down on it and knelt at her feet.

"I'm going to take off your shoes," he informed her.

She nodded numbly, her eyes fastened on him in wonderment. Thus began the ritual. Hank would have liked to dispense with her clothes as hastily as possible, but he cautioned himself against hurrying. He had never felt so clumsy. Bringing her to her feet, he fumbled with hooks and buttons until she was, at last, standing naked before him. He saw her shiver, although the room was quite warm. It occurred to him that a lady would feel uncomfortable standing naked in front of even her husband, so he quickly pulled down the bedspread and guided her between the sheets in deference to her modesty. In time she would lose her self-consciousness, but tonight he had to remember she was a virgin bride.

His own clothes were quickly discarded, and he soon joined Mary, being careful not to make any sudden rough moves. This could be terrible or wonderful for her; it all depended on how he handled it.

Then, to his utter astonishment he heard her say, "I'm not made out of china, Hank. I won't break, and I would so like for you to hold me."

His astonishment was replaced by throat-lumping joy. His arms went around her, and he drew her to him, pressing her length along his. The turgid proof of his arousal pressed against her softness. "Oh, my goodness!" she exclaimed softly. "Oh, my goodness! So this is how it feels. Harriet's books never did it justice. There's a lot we have to learn about each other."

"I love you so much, Mary."

"And I love you."

"You probably deserve a real gentleman who can give you a fine home. I think it's safe to say I'll never be a real gentleman, and I'm not too sure we'll ever have a fine home, but I promise you one thing. You could search all over the world and never find anyone who loves you the way I do."

"Oh, Hank... that's the most important thing, isn't it?"

He moved over her then, soothing, petting and kissing, until he could stand it no longer. He slipped a hand between her thighs, eliciting a gasp from her. "You tell me what to do," she whispered.

"Just whatever comes naturally."

Actually, there was a surprising lack of awkwardness. Hank knew he hurt her initially, but all he heard was a tiny whimper, then a moan. In no time at all they were moving in rhythm, matching each other gesture for gesture. Hank's release came sooner than he wanted, and he knew Mary had not reached completion, but perhaps that was to be expected the first time. The marriage bed was more complicated for a woman than for a man.

When his spasms had subsided, he rolled off her and cradled her in his arms. "Are you all right?"

"Of course I'm all right, silly. What did you expect?"

"I hurt you."

"Not much," she assured him, stretching and purring, then snuggling against him. "It wasn't nearly as bad as..."

"As you thought it was going to be, is that what you were going to say?" he asked with a chuckle.

"Well...girls talk. Some of the girls at the academy had older married sisters, and they loved to tell us all sorts of tales. Tonight was supposed to be something every bride dreads, but I didn't dread it. I thought it was actually very nice. Can we do it again?"

"After a bit. It takes a man a little while to...er, recover."

"What a shame. I don't feel like I have to 'recover' from anything."

"Mary, honey...trust you to be the unconventional virgin bride. Why don't you try to take a little nap? It's been a busy day."

Mary didn't feel the least like sleeping. She felt that she and Hank had just skimmed the surface, that there was so much more exploring and learning they had to do, and she was eager to begin. But she supposed that would have to wait. Beside her,

Hank had quickly succumbed to slumber, and within a minute, she, too, had fallen asleep.

MARY WOKE IN STAGES. Completely disoriented at first, she slowly adjusted to her surroundings. She had no idea what time it was, but the room lay in total darkness. Beside her, Hank still slept soundly.

Raising herself on an elbow, she stared down at him adoringly. In repose, his face looked boyish. *Maiden no more,* she thought in awe. *I'm a married woman!* She wished she were still in touch with Harriet. How she would have loved to tell her onetime best friend that she need fear nothing from her wedding night.

Mary lay down again and pulled the covers up under her chin. In all of her life she had never slept naked, and she didn't feel comfortable with it. Quietly sliding out of bed, she hurried to her bag to withdraw her lace-trimmed nightgown. After she'd slipped it over her head, she went back to the bed and waited for Hank to rouse.

Goodness, the bar downstairs was loud! She could hear the far-off but distinctive sound of piano music—"Alexander's Ragtime Band," if she wasn't mistaken. The music teacher at the academy had considered ragtime decadent, but Mary loved it. It was music she could tap her toes to. She lay very still and drummed the melody on her stomach.

And there was apparently a stairway somewhere nearby, on the other side of the wall. She could hear a steady stream of footsteps, some heavy, some light. And laughter—loud, raucous laughter, both masculine and feminine. Doors opened and closed noisily. She wondered how late the racket went on.

Just then Hank stirred beside her. "Mary?" he asked groggily.

She moved closer. "Yes, Hank. I'm here."

"Thank God. I was afraid I'd dreamed everything." He fumbled for her. "What are you wearing?"

"A nightgown. Feel it. It's soft as silk and has lace...."

"I'd rather feel you."

The gown was dispensed with, and Hank drew her close. For the next hour or so they explored each other's mysteries. And before it was over, Mary had experienced the most glorious rapture. Never would she have dreamed she could be so happy. She was going to make him the best wife a man ever had. Her uncle had been right—she didn't know how to do any of the things a wife was supposed to do. But she would learn.

"Hank?"

"What, hon?"

"What time are we going to leave in the morning?"

"Early. We'll have breakfast at Barney's, then light out."

"What do you know about this place called Prairie Gap?"

"Not much." What he knew was what little Jimmy had told him, and none of it was good. It wasn't really a town, just a settlement without amenities. Save for a small general store that served the area's ranchers and farmers, the nearest place to shop was Abilene. When he had wired Jimmy that he was bringing Mary with him and to please find them a place to stay, Jimmy's replying wire had been short and to the point.

HAVE YOU LOST YOUR MIND STOP WILL SEE WHAT I CAN DO STOP

So far, Hank mused, he wasn't doing so well as a husband. All he could do was hope and pray Jimmy came through for them and found something reasonably decent, something that wouldn't be so shoddy that he'd be embarrassed to ask Mary to live in it.

But he didn't wish that nearly as much as he hoped and prayed Mary, his love and the joy of his life, never learned she had spent her wedding night in a whorehouse.

THE FOLLOWING MORNING Hank and Mary left Slaterton after an early breakfast. What passed for the highway to Abilene was nothing more than a dirt road just wide enough for two buggies to pass, paralleling the Texas and Pacific tracks. Thick prairie grass brushed the tops of the automobile's running boards. When they reached the town, the scorching sun was high and mercilessly bright. Mary stopped in front of a mercantile store that had a portable gasoline pump in front.

"I'm almost sure we need to get gasoline, Hank," she said.

"We've got that extra can Duncan gave us."

"I know, but we really should save that for absolute emergencies. How much farther do you think we have to go?"

"I'm not sure, but someone inside might be able to tell me. I'll be right back."

Hank returned in a minute with a young clerk who filled the car's tank. His directions to Prairie Gap were sketchy at best. "Seems to me it's about five miles south of the town limits. Don't rightly recall, but if you turn left two blocks down thataway, you'll see the railroad crossing. Go over that, and you oughta see the place 'fore long. Ain't much there."

Mary had cautioned herself not to expect much of a place called Prairie Gap, and it was a good thing because "ain't much there" was an understatement. There were a few boarded-up buildings, a general store that was open for business and behind it a small frame house—belonging to the store's owner, she assumed. Driving on, she spotted some tents, a variety of vehicles and a small cabin. In the distance she could see a derrick in the process of being erected. Mary swallowed her dismay and fought to keep it from showing on her face. Not for the world would she let Hank know that her worst imaginings hadn't conjured up this. Where were they supposed to *live?*

She felt Hank stir beside her. "Mary, honey, you don't have to stay out here. We'll find you a place in Abilene. I didn't bring you out here to live in a tent."

"I know you didn't," she said, giving him her bravest smile. "*I* brought me out here, remember? And I'm not going to live in a room in Abilene while you spend most of the time out here, not if I can help it."

Pushing her foot down on the pedal, she drove them toward what at the moment seemed a very uncertain future.

CHAPTER SEVEN

Prairie Gap was Mary's baptism by fire. Jimmy Blue had commandeered the driller's cabin for them. The driller himself, the boss at a well site, slept in the doghouse beside the rig, and the others slept where they could, mostly in tents. Grandpa loved telling the story over the years. "There I was," he would say, "the greenest boll weevil in camp, but I was the only one with a roof over my head, a bed to sleep in and a sweet wife to keep me company."

Mary was the only woman there, and in the beginning she was the object of distrust. The men generally believed it was bad luck to have a woman near a drilling rig. She was lonely, but Grandpa told me more than once that she never complained, only set about learning to be a wife, with no skills and only the most rudimentary equipment. It was at Prairie Gap that she learned to cook, and being Mary, she tackled the chore with enthusiasm and determination, regarding it as just another challenge. It wasn't too long, according to Grandpa, before she was dishing up stew, beans and chicken-fried steak to the entire crew, thereby earning their respect, and even some grudging affection.

Of course Hank and Mary didn't stay in Prairie Gap long. Until the well came in. Then they were off again.

"DADDY?" a soft voice said.

J.T. looked up from his writing to see his daughter, Lynn, framed in the doorway. "Yes, honey. Come in."

Lynn crossed the room and took a chair facing her father's desk. "Are you still writing Grandpa Hank's biography?"

J.T. chuckled. "Sure appears to be just that, doesn't it? That poor fellow at the newspaper has his work cut out for him, editing this. Once I get started, I don't seem to be able to stop."

"You've been at it more than a week." Lynn frowned. "I miss him so much."

"I know you do, Lynn. We all do."

"Yes, but Grandpa Hank and I...well, there was something between us. Do you believe he was clairvoyant?"

J.T. made a rocking motion with his hand. "I...I've never been sure. So many of those prophecies of his could have been blind luck."

"No, they weren't," Lynn said. "He did see things no one else did." She paused a minute before saying, "I believed him because I have some of that in me, too."

J.T. looked startled. "You do?"

She nodded. "I'm forever seeing things that come to pass later on. Grandpa Hank was the only one I ever told that to, because I knew he'd believe me. And he did. We talked about it a lot this past year. I think it pleased him that someone in the family had inherited that from him."

"Lynn, you amaze me. I never suspected. And you never told your brothers, not Tyler, not even Cal? I thought you told Cal just about everything."

Lynn shrugged. "Oh...things change," she said a bit sadly. "Tyler, Cal and I have our own lives now. I can hardly remember the last time I really talked to Cal. It's incredible how much has changed in...oh, the past year and a half. Now Grandpa Hank's gone."

Silence settled over the room for a minute. Then, sighing, Lynn pushed herself out of the chair. "Well, I'll let you get back to what you're doing."

"Do you want to stay and talk a while?" J.T. asked, troubled by her pensive mood.

"No, I didn't really have anything to say. I think I'll go for a ride. Be sure and make Grandpa Hank sound interesting, Daddy."

"How could I do anything else? He *was* interesting."

"Talk to you later."

J.T. stared after her a minute before picking up his pen and continuing.

Hank and Mary made most of the booms in those wild and woolly years—along the Gulf Coast and up by the Red River. The master plot was always the same: in some remote, drought-stricken area where almost no one thought a drop of oil could be found, someone would persist and hit it big. Then the invasion would begin.

The same faces showed up at all the booms. In fact, when a field played out or a company decided to move on or rumor of a new boom circulated, the standard farewell was, "So long, boys. See you in the next boom."

Mary's beloved Model T was an early casualty of those years. It was simply too much trouble, so she reluctantly allowed Hank to sell it after he promised to buy another car when they were a little more settled—leaving her to wonder just when that would be. My mother, Emily, was born in early 1915, so besides cop-

ing with moving every time the notion struck
Hank, Mary had to try to raise an infant under conditions that were anything but desirable. Then came a place called Ranger....

AMERICA WAS at war. In a fit of patriotism mixed
with some male vanity, Hank had gone to the
nearest recruiting station to sign up for the army.
But after stripping to the buff and enduring the
physical, a tough-looking sergeant had said, "If
you wanna help Uncle Sam, son, you keep doing
what you're doing. He's gonna need every drop of
oil he can get."

So the war in Europe had turned oil prospecting
into big business, a vital part of the war effort. Holt
Petroleum was drilling a wildcat near Cisco in the
summer of 1917, and Mary and Emily were spending the duration of the drilling at the YH. "It'll save
you another move, honey," Hank had told Mary.
"Maybe your mama can come up to visit you."

"I don't like being away from you so long,"
Mary had said, but Hank hadn't missed the relief
on her face when she discovered she wasn't going to
have to secure temporary lodging for them in yet
another depressing town. That stabbed at his con-
science.

"I don't like leaving you either, Mary, and God
knows I'm gonna miss you somethin' fierce, but

you need a rest. You've been lookin' kinda peaked and tired lately.''

So he had left his wife and daughter at the ranch, and he and Jimmy Blue shared a room at the Mobley Hotel in Cisco. In those days Hank was doing the meanest kind of backbreaking labor, but he was learning. There wasn't much about working a rig he didn't know by now, and he and Jimmy had never given up hope that they would be in business for themselves one day. It was Jimmy who first suggested that Ranger might be the place where they could begin making their fortune.

The two friends were having coffee in the hotel on one of their rare mornings off. ''Why Ranger?'' Hank asked. The town wasn't far away. He had been there, and it didn't seem much different from all the other farm towns he had seen.

''Because the Texas and Pacific Coal Company has leased twenty-five thousand acres there and is drilling a well on a farm owned by a fellow named McCleskey. That tells me something.''

Hank never knew how Jimmy became privy to so much inside information, but little went on in the oil patch that the geologist wasn't aware of.

''I'm telling you, Hank, I feel this one. If we could just get hold of some leases.''

''And a rig...and a crew,'' Hank reminded him.

''Yeah, I know. And some cash. That most of all. Plenty of people have gotten land, only to find

out they didn't have the money to develop it."
Jimmy brooded in silence a minute before saying,
"I sure am ready to leave Holt, for more reasons
than one. I heard some news this morning that
didn't exactly make me want to break out into
song."

"Oh?"

"The word is that Elver's about to turn the field
operations over to his kid, Garmon."

Hank digested that. "Well, guess if I was Elver
and had a son, that's what I'd do, too. Just take it
easy for a spell and spend some of my money."

"Have you ever met Garmon?"

"No." Hank had never met any of Elver's family. In fact, he hadn't seen Elver himself more than
a dozen times. The Holts, he'd heard, resided in a
Fort Worth mansion where they enjoyed all the
good things in life that owning oil was beginning to
provide the fortunate few.

"He was educated at Harvard or Yale...or
maybe it was Princeton. One of those schools."

"Is he a chip off the old block?" Hank asked.
"Like Elver? Lucky...and good at finding oil?"

Jimmy snorted. "Garmon Holt couldn't find his
own ass with both hands and a lantern."

Hank chuckled. "Guess he doesn't have to as
long as Elver's his daddy."

"Seems he's been down in South Texas oversee-
ing the Holt interests there, but now his daddy

thinks he ought to come up here where the action is." Jimmy made a scoffing sound. "Fine lot of good that Eastern dude's going to do us. Just thinking about working for Garmon makes me want to throw up. When you meet him you'll see what I mean."

Hank didn't have to wait long to meet the Holt heir. Three days later a sleek Hudson town car drove up to the well site, and two men got out. One was Elver, and he was accompanied by a man in his mid-twenties. Hank rightly assumed the young man was Elver's son. They didn't look as though they could be even remotely related, much less father and son. Elver was a big man—not fat, just big— with heavy brows and big jowls. Garmon Holt was tall, slender and possessed of the pretty-boy good looks that Hank had never been able to consider masculine. He was dressed in a starched white shirt and tailored dark trousers and presented a sharp contrast to the men in their stained khakis.

Elver introduced his son, then Garmon mingled, shaking hands with the crew. His manicured nails, smooth hands and indifferent handshake did nothing to elevate Hank's opinion of him.

Nor did anything else Garmon did during the ensuing weeks. He was expert at staying away from anything that might get his hands dirty. He left the site promptly at five o'clock every afternoon and returned to the Mobley Hotel, not showing up again until nine or ten the following morning. Word had it that Garmon was awfully fond of whiskey and women, and he'd certainly come to the right place for both. He went through the motions of being one of the men and even took to calling Hank "ol' buddy," but his only real concession to his new surroundings was to exchange his starched white shirts for starched khakis.

However, Hank was one to give credit where credit was due. Garmon didn't know how to do one damn thing that was of any value around a rig, and he was smart enough to stay out of the way of those who did.

The main thing Garmon's presence at the site did for Hank was to remind him of the inequities of various stations in life. Elver's son would have everything without having to work for it, while Hank and his kind would scratch and claw for every step up the ladder. Unbidden and unwanted, memories of Billie Jean Surratt flashed through his mind, something that hadn't happened since he married Mary, and the old resentment briefly flared.

In the meantime, Jimmy kept abreast of everything that was happening on the McCleskey farm near Ranger. The geologist was sitting in a café having lunch one day when a young boy of about ten rushed in hollering that something had gone wrong at the McCleskey well. "There's a terrible noise, like the whole world's turned inside out or something!'' he cried. Almost the entire town emptied within seconds as everyone raced to the well. The terrible noise, of course, was the sound of oil gushing to the surface. Jimmy immediately drove to Cisco. What he and Hank had been waiting for had finally happened.

BY WEEK'S END, people were streaming into the area on or in anything that could be ridden or driven. The Mobley Hotel lobby became a sort of unofficial stock exchange while fortune seekers pondered their next moves. Among them were a young roustabout and a geologist.

What Hank and Jimmy needed more than anything was a lease and the money to develop it. Therefore, they decided the best thing they could do was hang around the Mobley and listen. Jimmy spent most of his time there since, as the ''consultant,'' he had little to do at the well site. When Hank wasn't working, he joined his friend.

That was how they happened to overhear a conversation among a group of men who introduced themselves around the lobby as investors from Kansas City. Nothing they said seemed of much interest until they mentioned a name. Ben Coker. Jimmy knew of Coker.

''Jimmy, how in hell do you know all these people?'' Hank wanted to know.

"I move around, talk to people and listen. Coker's a rancher with about two thousand acres south of here. He's just about starving, like all the others since the drought hit. He'd like to have an oil well or two, but he doesn't trust oilers. Says they're a shifty lot, and he's afraid he couldn't get an honest deal out of one."

Hank thought about that a minute. "Wonder how he'd feel about a poor ol' cowpoke who's just tryin' to better himself?"

"You?" Jimmy asked with a grin.

"Me. Jimmy, how much money you got in the bank?"

"Maybe a thousand."

"Yeah, that's about what I have. 'Course, it's Mary's, too, but... Tell you what. You go draw yours out in small bills. Just leave enough in to keep the account open. I'll do the same." Hank stood and kicked back his chair with his heel. "Come on, friend. As my daddy used to say, daylight's wastin'."

"I hope to hell you know what you're doing," Jimmy said as he followed Hank out of the lobby.

"So do I."

"Want me to go with you?"

"Nope. Coker might not trust geologists, either, and there's no way you could ever pass for a cowpoke, my friend."

FOLLOWING Jimmy's instructions, Hank rode out
of town and south of Ranger. Before leaving the
hotel he had fished out some of his cowboy garb
left over from his days at the YH. The pants and
shirt were worn, the hat stained, and the boots
scuffed. He still sat a horse well, so he hoped he
looked the very picture of a working cowhand.

Jimmy had said that Coker would probably jump
at three dollars an acre. If that was true, Hank figured the rancher would be able to get that anywhere, so he planned to offer him four, or roughly
four times what he and Jimmy together had. If that
didn't work, he'd go to five. Caution had no place
in the oil business.

The gate to the Coker ranch was nothing more
than a gap in the barbed-wire fence. Ahead, Hank
could see a modest bungalow. A screened veranda
ran all the way around it. Behind it, a windmill
creaked and groaned as the wind turned its wheel
and poured water into a wooden storage tank.
Chickens foraged on a pitiful patch of Bermuda
grass that was struggling mightily to survive without water. The place spoke of little in the way of
creature comforts. If anyone could use an oil well,
Hank mused, Coker could.

A spare, weathered man of about fifty sat in a
cowhide rocker on the veranda. Hank rode unhurriedly to the hitching post that stood in front of the

house, but he knew better than to dismount without being invited to.

"Howdy," he said, touching the brim of his hat with a finger.

"Howdy," the man replied in a rasping voice, peering at him through the screen. "What kin I do fer ya?"

"I'm looking for Mr. Coker."

"Ya found him."

"My name's Hank Travis, Mr. Coker. I came out here with a little business proposition for you. I'd like a few minutes of your time."

Coker squinted as he looked his visitor up and down, then apparently decided Hank looked all right. "Might as well sit a spell since ya come all the way out here."

Hank dismounted, tethered his horse and climbed the steps. He opened the screen door and noticed there was no other chair available, so he propped his rump against the veranda's railing and crossed his arms over his chest. "Looks like it's gonna be another hot one," he said.

"Ya coulda said thet ever' day fer the past six months. Things are 'bout to change, though."

"Oh?"

"Drought's gonna end purty soon."

"That must be good news for you."

Coker scratched his chin. "Might be too late fer me."

It was the opening Hank had been waiting for. "Well, sir, if that's true, you just might be interested in what I have to say." He squatted down on his haunches in true cowboy fashion. "You see, I'm just a cowpoke who's managed to put together a little money over the years, and I'd like to do something with it. I don't have to tell you that it's getting harder and harder to make a livin' in ranchin', so not many spreads are hirin'."

Coker nodded sagely but said nothing.

"Well, like I said, I have a little money, and I was thinking about doin' some oil prospectin' with it."

Coker cackled. "You and ever' other fellow I met lately. Know anythin' about the oil bi'ness, son?"

"A little bit . . . but I've got a partner who knows it all." Hank didn't think he was misrepresenting the facts *too* much. "What we have in mind, sir, is offering to lease your property for the purpose of oil prospecting. The price we have in mind is . . . oh, four dollars an acre . . . and an eighth override."

"A what?"

"Every eight barrels that come out of the ground, one is yours. 'Course we know you wouldn't have the first thing to do with a barrel of oil, so your eighth would be paid to you as royalty." He quickly gauged Coker's reaction.

"Well, I'll be goddamned!"

"Haven't you been offered an override before, Mr. Coker?"

"Never heard tell o' such."

"Sounds to me like you've been talkin' to the wrong people."

"Thet's what I always figured."

So now Hank knew he had topped any other offers the rancher had received. He reached into his hip pocket with a small flourish and withdrew the cash he and Jimmy had put together. A little less than two thousand dollars in small bills made quite a wad. Coker's eyes almost popped out of his head.

"You can rest assured that this is a fair-and-square deal, sir. Are you interested?"

"Mebbe. How you plannin' on payin'?"

"Cash when you sign the lease. Any royalty payments due you will be in the form of company checks."

Coker didn't seem to be able to take his eyes off the wad of bills in Hank's hand. "What do I hafta do to git thet money?"

Hank reached in his shirt pocket for the lease agreement Jimmy had hastily drawn up. "Just sign this. It's permission for anyone who holds this lease to drill for oil on your property for the next ten years."

"What happens if ya don't find nuthin'?"

"If no oil has been found when the lease expires, the mineral rights will revert to you, and you can sell them to the highest bidder."

Coker chuckled. "If'n oil ain't bin found in ten years, reckon there's none down there. Gimme that paper." He couldn't sign it fast enough.

With great deliberation, Hank pretended to count the bills, though he knew to the dollar what was there. When he finished, he frowned. "Well, damn, Mr. Coker, I don't have near as much cash on me as I thought. A little under two thousand. Would you consider taking my personal check for the remainder?"

"No! I don't like checks."

"Too bad. I'm sure sorry about this." Hank rolled up the bills and started to stuff them back into his hip pocket. "Guess we'll just have to finish this deal tomorrow after I can get to the bank."

Coker gave a start. "Now, wait a goddanged minute. Not so fast. I s'pose... well, I s'pose I kin take your check since ya seem like an honest fella. Sure I can cash it tomorrow?"

"Of course." Hank didn't consider that a lie. If things went the way he hoped they would, Coker would be able to cash that check tomorrow, and he and Jimmy would have money to spare. And if they didn't... well, he'd have to worry about that when the time came.

"Then I'll just take thet almost-two-thousand along with yer check." Coker kept staring at the bills. "Thet thar's more cash money than I ever seen at one time."

Hank handed over the cash, along with a very worthless check for six thousand dollars and some change. Then, not wanting to appear too anxious to get the hell out of there, he spent a few minutes passing the time with the old rancher. But once they'd said their goodbyes, he rode as fast as he could back to Cisco, arriving at the Mobley around five o'clock, just before dinner when the lobby was at its busiest.

Jimmy wasn't there or in their room, and Hank felt that time was of the essence. He changed clothes and returned to the lobby, where he mingled and eavesdropped on conversations. Within an hour he had peddled the Coker leases for sixteen thousand dollars, paid for with a certified check from an investment firm in Kansas City. Hank's heart was beating so wildly he thought it would burst inside his chest. An eight-thousand-dollar profit for half a day's effort!

Jimmy finally showed up and found his partner pacing the floor and smoking cigarette after cigarette. When he heard the news, he was impressed. "I thought you were whistling in the wind. I sure didn't think you could do it."

"This is the way we're gonna do it, Jimmy," Hank said excitedly. "This is the way we're gonna get enough money together to drill us a wildcat. This hotel's just full of fellows from somewhere else, people who don't know beans about doing business with old farmers and ranchers. But I can 'cause I've been one of 'em. I'm gonna lease everything I can get my hands on for four or five dollars an acre, then sell it to the city slickers for three times that much."

Jimmy looked at him askance. "You're going to be a lease hound?" In the oil business, that was not a highly regarded occupation.

"Just temporarily, just until we have our stake."

"Chasing leases is going to be kinda hard with you working for Elver, isn't it?"

"I'm quittin' Elver. Been wantin' to ever since that ass Garmon got to be boss, so I'm doin' it."

"When?"

"In the morning, right after I go to the bank and cover one very hot check."

Jimmy let out a little whistle. "That's a bit risky."

"Jimmy, you know of anyone in this business who hasn't taken a big risk at one time or another?" Hank wasn't nearly as cocky and self-confident as he sounded. For one thing, he hated telling Mary he was yanking her security out from under her. Time was, before Emily's birth, when his wife was the biggest risk-taker of all. But she was a mother now and looked at a lot of things differently. "Come on, friend, let's go down to dinner and talk about the future. Hell, we might be millionaires in a month's time."

They weren't, of course, but the newly formed Travis-Blue Production and Exploration Company was worth a lot of money, six figures, even though it had neither produced nor explored anything. And it was largely due to Hank's success in securing leases, which he later sold for far more than he'd given for them. Along the way, he kept the ones Jimmy considered the choicest for Travis-Blue.

At last they were ready to drill their own wildcat. They obtained a "poor boy" rig from a disgruntled operator who had gone broke and lured a driller and a couple of roughnecks away from Holt. They were only days away from making hole when Hank astonished Jimmy by telling him to wait a while.

"Wait?" the geologist asked. "What for?"

"For me to go to the YH and get Mary and Emily. I just feel luckier when they're with me. And while I'm gone, find a house for us to rent."

"Here in Cisco?"

Hank shook his head. "In Ranger. I want to be close to the action."

"What am I going to find to rent in that burg?"

"You'll find something. Make it decent. See you in a week, friend."

MARY WAS STANDING at the window of her old bedroom on the second floor of the ranch house when she saw him riding through the gate. Stifling a whoop so as not to disturb the sleeping Emily, she raced out of the room, down the stairs and out onto the porch, skirt flying. Seeing her, Hank quickened his horse's pace. He slid out of the saddle, tethered the animal and scooped Mary up in his arms, seemingly in one swift motion.

"Hot damn, it's good to see you, honey! I've missed you something awful."

"And I've missed you, Hank. Come inside."

The big house was shuttered against the afternoon heat. Inside it was cool, dim and utterly quiet. "Where's Duncan?" Hank asked.

"In town. I don't expect him back for hours." Taking his hand, Mary led him upstairs and into her bedroom, pressing a finger against her lips as she indicated Emily asleep in her crib.

"Won't we wake her?" Hank whispered.

She shook her head. "Nothing wakes her. She'll sleep for another hour."

Hank peered over the crib and smiled. "Is it my imagination or has she grown an inch?"

"It's not your imagination." Mary slid her arms up his chest and locked her hands behind his neck. "It's so wonderful to have you back with us. Want to get comfortable?"

Hank placed a lingering kiss on her lips, then smiled at her adoringly. "Sure we won't wake up the scamp?"

"I'm sure." There were few preliminaries. They were undressed and in bed within seconds, and they made love with the ease of longtime lovers, sweetly and unhurriedly. In the golden aftermath, they lay wound around each other, totally happy and completed. "Mary, you're wonderful," Hank said. "I swear I'm going to try to find more time for just the two of us."

"Uh-huh," she said lazily. "I've heard *that* before."

"No, I'm serious. Damned if I don't think it's time for a second honeymoon."

"Honeymoon? Let's see, what's that?" she teased. "Oh, I remember. I spent the first one in Prairie Gap, as I recall, and my wedding night in a brothel."

Hank gasped, bolted upright and looked down at her. "Mary! You . . . knew?"

"Well, I didn't know it that night, but since then I've put two and two together."

"Honey, I just hated that worse than anything, but we were in a real fix. I'm sorry."

"Don't be. It made my wedding night rather unique, don't you think? You were quite resourceful to come up with Gracie's."

Hank shook his head in wonder. "I guess you'll never stop amazing me. Maybe that's why being married to you is such fun." He sank down beside her again.

Contentedly, Mary lay in his arms for a minute before asking, "Are you taking us back with you?"

"Yeah. And . . . I have something to tell you."

Mary tensed. She knew that tone of voice so well. "What is it?"

"I've quit Holt."

A few seconds of heavy silence ensued. Then Mary casually said, "Oh? What brought that on?"

Quickly he told her everything that had happened since he'd last seen her. Mary listened quietly, as though he was telling her a bit of gossip instead of talking about their future. At that moment she felt as insecure as she had back in Prairie Gap.

"Well, it's what you've always wanted," she finally said, then rolled out of bed and began dressing.

"Mad?"

"No."

"Not even disappointed?"

"Of course not. It will be an adventure. When are we leaving?"

"Can you leave in the morning? We're about ready to make hole."

"In the morning it is."

"Jimmy's getting us a house, and as soon as we're settled in, we'll get us another car. Ranger's a big boom, honey. A really big one."

Aren't they all? Mary crossed the room and looked down at her sleeping daughter. She supposed it was too much to hope that this boom lasted a while. Right now, with Emily only a baby, moving every time the mood struck Hank didn't affect their family life, but someday it would. Someday Emily would need a real home, friends and something resembling roots. What then?

CHAPTER EIGHT

MUD AND BLOOD, Mary thought, as she stared out
the window at the pouring rain. The drought had
broken with a bang, leaving them with the most
dismal October she had ever lived through. The
farmers and ranchers were thrilled, of course, but
the rains were a nightmare for everyone else.

The streets of Ranger were quagmires, and the
floors of all the stores had an inch of mud on them.
Mary had forgotten what it was like to wear pretty
shoes. She and every woman in town wore heavy
rubber boots when outdoors. The hems of all her
dresses were a dirty brown that no amount of
washing could remove. Since coming to Ranger,
Hank had bought a secondhand Packard, and it
was equipped with a heavy chain for being towed
and a shovel for digging out of the mire. But horses
definitely had their advantage in the muck.

Mary turned from the window and sighed. There
was very little that was pleasant about Ranger. It
was just like all the other places she and Hank had
been, not far removed from a Tombstone or Dodge

City. Violence seemed to stalk the boom towns like a starving coyote after a prairie dog. Dead bodies didn't even create any excitement, and murderers were rarely caught. The ones who were seldom were prosecuted. Saloons and brothels were open for business twenty-four hours a day, and there were areas in town where ladies simply did not go.

It often amazed her that her kindhearted, thoughtful husband just flourished in such surroundings, though she suspected Hank of not being the same person on the well site that he was at home. He was forever having to watch his language around Emily, but Mary imagined no such courtesy was shown around the well.

The wildcat he and Jimmy were drilling had become an obsession with him. He could scarcely drag himself away from it, and Mary worried constantly that he didn't eat properly or get enough rest.

However, something else worried her even more. Hank and Jimmy talked about becoming millionaires, but Mary wondered if money was really the force that drove her husband. She suspected it was the chase. Oilmen referred to their business as "the game," and that was what it was more than anything, it seemed to her. That being the case, she couldn't see Hank ever settling down for long, no matter how much money he made.

She surprised herself sometimes. Once she had sworn that she would never depend on someone else for her well-being and happiness. When she had married Hank, she hadn't considered it giving up her independence, and she still didn't. But her energies had been channeled in other directions. Now Hank and Emily were her world, and more than anything, she wanted that world to have some stability.

Just then she heard a familiar sound. Emily was waking from her nap. Turning, Mary rushed to the crib. "Here, darling," she said, picking up the child and cradling her head in the curve of her shoulder. "I'll bet you're wet. Mercy, I wish those diapers would dry. I'm just about out of clean ones. After I change you, I'll get you some milk and a cookie."

The house Jimmy had rented for them was exceptionally nice for Ranger. On a quiet side street, it had two big, high-ceilinged bedrooms, a bathroom between them, a living room and a huge farmhouse-type kitchen with a round table and chairs. Mary'd had a wonderful time decorating it, but the decor could hardly be appreciated now. Clotheslines had been strung throughout the house, and diapers and clothes hung from all of them. *Lord, I wish this blasted rain would end,* she thought as she carried Emily to the kitchen. She longed for the smell of sunshine-dried clothes again.

But the rain and the drying clothes seemed to keep her pesky affliction at bay. She hadn't had a bout of coughing of any consequence since the drought broke.

Emily was changed, her dark curly hair brushed, and she snuggled in her mother's lap, enjoying her afternap snack. Mary sat at the kitchen table, staring out the window over her daughter's head. Once Emily was finished, she would play, and Mary would play with her or read to her or to herself. She found herself wishing Hank would show up for supper, but he rarely did. Sometimes when the loneliness threatened to overwhelm her, Mary would remind herself that the rain wouldn't last forever, that the well would either come in or be plugged, that there was tomorrow and the next day. She wasn't really as far from civilization as it sometimes seemed, and she had a husband who loved her, a darling daughter, a roof over her head and plenty of food on the table. She needed to count her blessings.

MARY HAD BEEN ASLEEP for hours when she heard the noise. Turning her head on the pillow, she looked at the clock. "Is that you, Hank?"

The other side of the mattress sagged under his weight. "Is there somebody else you might be expecting to crawl into bed with you at four in the morning?"

Chuckling, Mary reached for him. "Hmm, you smell nice."

"I stopped at the bathhouse in town before coming home. Didn't want to wake you and the babe, and I know how you feel about the smell of crude." He pulled her close and kissed her temple. "God, I love the way your hair feels."

"I know." She took special care with her crowning glory because Hank liked it so much. "How are things at the well?"

"We passed three thousand feet today."

"Is that good?"

"We're gettin' close to where Jimmy thinks we oughta hit. Another few days and we'll know if we have a well or a duster."

"You sound concerned."

"Just impatient."

Mary dovetailed her body against his and smiled. "You know, today I was thinking of what all I'd like to do to the house when spring comes. I'm going to plant some flowers—snapdragons and hollyhocks like we had at the farm. And if you'll dig me a garden, I could learn to grow tomatoes and corn and green beans. Wouldn't it be wonderful to have really fresh vegetables in the summer instead of those tinned things?"

She paused, waiting for his reply, but his steady, shallow breathing told her he was asleep. Sighing, she moved away from him slightly, plumped her pillow and tried to get comfortable. It was useless, however. She had been in bed for more than five hours. She'd never get back to sleep.

After quietly crawling out of bed, she slipped on her robe and crossed the hall to look in on Emily. When her daughter was asleep she looked like an angel, which she wasn't, by any means. She was as spirited as a colt and had a temper that often startled her mother. Once, when Mary had commented to Hank that Emily was going to be a handful when she got older, he had smiled and said, "Do tell. Who do you suppose she got that from?"

Leaving Emily's room, Mary headed to the kitchen and poured a glass of milk, then carried it into the living room. The rain had stopped sometime around sundown and hadn't started up again. Peeking out the window, she saw that the moon was out. In moonlight, even the streets of Ranger took on a peaceful look.

She had no idea how long she had been standing at the window when she heard a noise from the back of the house. Frowning, she hurried into the bedroom and found Hank out of bed, struggling to put his trousers on.

"What are you doing?" she demanded incredulously.

"I've got to get out to the well," he said, zipping up his fly and reaching for his shirt.

"You just got in from the well!"

"I gotta go, Mary. Somethin' bad's about to happen."

"Hank . . . are you still asleep? What is this? Did you have a bad dream? Just get back in bed. Everything's fine." Mary moved toward him.

"I gotta go, honey. Believe me."

"I don't understand this!"

"I know you don't, and I don't have time to explain. Just trust me."

Mary took a step backward, her hand on her chest. She was frightened, but she knew Hank. He was never irrational. He didn't have flights of fancy. And right now he was scared; that much she could see. If he thought something bad was going to happen, she feared something bad was going to happen. So she stood by helplessly and watched as he dressed. Once his boots were on, he made for the front door.

Mary was hard on his heels. "Hank, don't you dare let anything happen to you," she said, fighting back tears.

He stopped and kissed her, caressing her cheek. "Nothing's going to happen to me, honey. I'm just gonna see to it that nothing happens to anyone else."

Then he was gone.

HANK CURSED the Packard as it bounced over the rutted open land. What he wouldn't have given for a high-spirited horse at that moment. He didn't bother with roads, just lit out as the crow flies. With all the rain, open grassy prairie was more navigable than the rutted roads anyway. About half a mile from the rig, he parked the car and began to run. As soon as he got near enough, he started yelling, and he had developed some powerful lungs after years of trying to make himself heard over the roar of the drill.

"Shut 'er down!" he cried. "Get off that floor!"

Heads turned in his direction. "Shut it down and run, dammit! I'm tellin' you—*run!*"

Maybe it was the panic the others heard in his voice. Maybe they were simply used to doing what Hank said. Whatever the reason, the floor was abandoned in the blink of an eye. Anyone passing by would have been treated to the sight of a bunch of khaki-clad oilers running pell-mell across the dark prairie for no apparent reason.

Then there was a reason—a sharp hissing sound, then a roar followed quickly by an explosion. A great ball of fire rolled up the derrick; then the whole thing blew apart. The running men miraculously reached safety before the billowing flame reduced everything to fiery rubble. At the automobile, they turned as one to stare at what seconds ago had been a tall derrick.

"My God!" someone cried.

"How'd ya know, Hank?" another asked.

"I...don't know. Earlier when I was working on the floor, I just kept...well, hearing something that didn't sound quite right to me, nothin' I could give a name to. It sorta got to eatin' on me once I got home."

There was no way he was going to try to explain to these men that he had "seen" the fire before it happened. Sometimes the things he saw scared the hell out of him. The incredible thing was—he had seen it just the way it happened, that ball of fire shinnying up the derrick right before the explosion sent everything into oblivion. He was shaking all over.

The men gathered around Hank, mouths agape. "You saved all our lives!" one of them said.

"I'm just glad I got here in time. Now, come on, fellows, I'll take you to town." For the time being he wouldn't allow himself to dwell on everything that had just gone up in smoke.

THE EXPLOSION had rattled practically every window in town. Mary had not returned to bed after Hank left but had paced the floor, worry knotting her stomach. When she heard the explosion, she let out a cry and rushed out onto the front porch. Lights were coming on in houses all along the street, and people were venturing out. A cacophony of voices sounded in the predawn air.

Mary sank to the porch steps. *Hank's not out there,* she thought in desperation. *He's not at that well,* even though she was sure he was. She had been around the business long enough to know there were a dozen ways to get hurt or killed around a derrick, but the worst thing that could happen at a well was fire. Tears streamed down her cheeks. The only thing that kept her from breaking down altogether was the sound of Emily's voice as she woke. She musn't upset the little girl, who was so attuned to her mother's moods.

Somehow Mary got Emily dressed and fed, though she couldn't remember actually doing so. She had just finished when the front door opened and Hank walked in.

"Oh, thank God!" she cried, rushing toward him and hugging him ferociously.

"The well's gone, honey," he said dejectedly.

"Forget the well. You're safe."

"And considerably poorer."

Mary stepped back. He looked as though the world had just ended. "Was anybody hurt?"

Hank shook his head. "I'm going to make coffee," he said as he reached down to rumple Emily's hair. The child held out her arms, and he bent to scoop her up.

"I'll make the coffee," Mary said. "Emily wants you to hold her. She hardly ever sees you. Come on in the kitchen, you two. Don't you want breakfast, Hank?''

"Just coffee for now. I don't think I could eat a bite. My stomach's got some settlin' down to do first.''

Mary put water on to boil and took a tin of coffee out of the cupboard while Hank sat at the table and held Emily in his lap. ''How'd you know, Hank?'' Mary asked. ''How did you know about the well?''

''It's not easy to explain. Sometimes I just see things that are going to happen. I've been doing it all my life.''

''How come we've been married all this time and this is the first I've heard about it?'' The entire incident had left Mary with an eerie, confused feeling.

''I don't know. It's been a long time since I've had one of these visions. They used to worry me, but today I'm countin' my blessings. At least that sorry son of a . . . that sorry well didn't hurt anyone.''

''The things you see . . . is that why you were so sure we were going to have a daughter instead of a son?''

''I guess so.'' He chucked Emily under the chin.

The water was boiling. Mary threw in some coffee grounds, gave the pot a quick stir, then set it on the back of the stove.

"Hank?"

"Yeah, honey."

"Sometimes I wish...well, I wish you would give some thought to going into well servicing or oil field supply or something. There are dozens of ways to make a good living in the oil business. It doesn't have to be on a rig."

"You mean...rework some other fellow's rig? Sell some pipe to a real oiler?"

The tone of his voice told Mary just how that idea struck him. "It was just a thought," she said, standing and moving toward the stove. She was getting cups out of the cabinet when there was a knock on the front door. When she answered it, Mary found Jimmy Blue standing there, looking shaken.

"Is Hank all right?" he asked.

Mary nodded. "Come in, Jimmy. You're in time for coffee."

He followed her into the kitchen, and when he saw Hank he said, "You're the prettiest damn sight I ever laid eyes on. Did anybody get hurt?"

Hank shook his head. "Just our bank account. I'd like to say we'll have better luck next time, but I'm not sure there'll be a next time."

"What happened?"

"Don't know for sure. Guess we hit a pocket of gas."

"Damn gas," Jimmy muttered. "Too bad there's no market for the stuff, because there sure is a hell of a lot of it out here." He sank into the chair opposite Hank and shook his head wearily. "You know, some folks just aren't meant to have a lot of money, and I'm afraid I'm one of them."

"Yeah, maybe the good Lord means for me to always work for the other man." Hank looked at his friend. "You're lucky you have an education. You can always find work."

"What are *you* going to do?" Jimmy asked with concern.

Hank shrugged. "I don't know. Tuck my tail between my legs and ask that jerk Garmon to give me my old job back."

Mary had been listening to this exchange. She set their coffee in front of them and placed her hands on her hips. "The two of you still own a lot of leases, don't you?"

"A bunch," Hank said, "but now there's no money to develop them."

"Then I suggest you get your chins off your chests and start at the beginning. Sell enough leases to pay for your next well."

Hank and Jimmy looked at each other, then at Mary. "You mean, you'd take another chance?"

"I don't see any alternative, do you? Come on, Emily, let's go get some of your toys. You can play while I wash yet another pile of dirty diapers."

Mother and daughter left the room, and the men sat sipping coffee in silence for a minute. There were moments when Hank didn't know what to make of his wife. At a time like this, most women would be crying and wringing their hands. That would have been understandable. But Mary had simply come up with a solution on the spot. He supposed he should admire her for that, and he often did. But there were other times, like now, when she was so overwhelming that she terrified him a little.

"You know, she's probably right," Jimmy said. "I don't see any other way to recover our loss."

"Damn if I don't hate to give up those leases. Some of 'em are the best ones in the county."

"But some are better than others," Jimmy said, "and they're the ones we'll keep. We won't have any trouble getting top dollar for the rest."

"Do you really want to start all over?"

"You bet."

"Then you decide which leases we keep. I'll go out and peddle the rest." Hank paused to chuckle unmirthfully. "This sure is a crazy way to make a living."

"Yeah. But nobody ever said it was going to be easy."

"What if the next one is a duster...or another gas well?"

"Then you and I, friend, will have the reputation of being snake-bit. Nobody will want to work for us or give us credit or anything. Guess we'll just have to deal with that when the time comes. Right now we have work to do."

IT TOOK HANK less than a week to sell enough leases to put Travis-Blue back in business. Two months later they drilled their first producing well, and within a year's time, they owned four. Travis-Blue had become a big-time player with a good reputation, and that meant everything in the oil business. They decided to throw caution to the wind, and bought a spanking new rig, renting out the old poor-boy to small operators. The deals that came their way quadrupled. They had connections. Hank and Jimmy *belonged*.

Hank rented a bigger house on the outskirts of town, a two-story Victorian with an enormous fenced-in yard for Emily. He also bought Mary a fancy new hand-cranked laundry machine—a huge tub on four legs with a wringer attached. Mary thought it ironic that she acquired the splendid invention just as Emily left diapers.

That Christmas, Hank sent Mary's mother and brothers train tickets so they could come for a visit, and Duncan joined them. It tickled him to death to be able to show everyone that he had done right by Mary after all.

And he'd taken care of his own family. The old farm had always been just a step away from foreclosure, but it never would be again, thanks to Hank. Nor would his parents want for anything. Knowing that was a good feeling.

Mary never mentioned well servicing or the oil field supply business again, and the years in Ranger fairly flew by. She joined a group of concerned women who called themselves Citizens for a Better Community. They wanted stricter law enforcement and better schools, but their demands fell on deaf ears at first. Then the United States government unwittingly stepped in and helped their crusade.

In 1920, the eighteenth and nineteenth amendments to the constitution were passed. The first banned the production, sale and consumption of alcoholic beverages; the second gave women the vote. Now the gin mills were against the law, and women could vote for city and county officials. They could no longer be ignored. Of course Prohibition didn't end the liquor trade, but it did drive it out of sight . . . sort of. And the women's votes didn't abolish lawlessness, but lawbreakers were sometimes more thoroughly prosecuted than formerly by a sheriff eyeing re-election.

Little by little, changes came.

ON A BRIGHT SPRING afternoon in 1923, Hank sat with Jimmy in one of Ranger's legendary watering holes. Now, of course, it was called a coffeehouse, though one could order one's coffee "with," and that didn't mean with cream and sugar. Jimmy had taken to dressing like a Wall Street broker, but riches could only change Hank so much. He still wore khakis and still hung out at the wells as in the old days. Word around the oil patch was that he was a good man to work for because he wasn't afraid of work himself.

Jimmy had just returned from two weeks in far West Texas, and he was full of excitement. From the breast pocket of his suit, he produced a map, which he spread out on the table. "I've got something I want you to see. Out here," he said, tapping the map with his finger, "is where I've been. A place called Rimrock, and it's busting its britches."

Hank frowned as he studied the map. "Good Lord, Jimmy! Aren't there still Comanches that far out?"

Jimmy smiled. "All gone. You know about the Santa Rita."

Hank nodded. News of big strikes had a way of traveling around the oil business, particularly when they opened up an undeveloped area. Especially if they were found by a bunch of amateurs with more blind luck than good sense. Word was that some

Eastern investors had named the well after the patron saint of the impossible, but yarns like that were thick in the oil patch, and Hank figured maybe a third of them had any fact attached to them.

"It's taken a while, but now it's like firecrackers on a string, Hank," Jimmy said, his eyes alive. "McCamey, Crane, Winkler...and that's just the beginning, I promise. Drilling for oil out there isn't much more difficult than digging a hole in the ground. What they've done is open the Permian Basin."

"The what?"

"The Permian Basin. It's a formation geologists have known about for years. I'm telling you, Hank, that Basin is still going to be producing when your grandchildren are grown."

An old familiar feeling raced through Hank's veins. "So?"

"So I think Travis-Blue ought to jump in head-first."

Hank had been fighting the itch for more than a year, fighting it something fierce because he didn't want Mary to suspect he thought it was time to move on. She was awfully content with their lives right now. She and her little band of women probably had more to do with what went on in the town than the mayor and the sheriff put together. "When were you thinking about leaving?"

"Immediately."

"I got a wife and kid. It takes them a while to get their stuff together."

"We can't wait too long, Hank."

He nodded. "I'll talk to Mary tonight."

"By the way," Jimmy added, "Holt's going into the Basin in a big way. I ran into Garmon in Rimrock. He's in charge of setting up their operation there."

"Did you give him my love?"

"I met his wife, too."

"He's married? I'd sure as hell like to meet a gal who'd want to marry Garmon."

"She's a looker, someone he met when he was working in South Texas." Jimmy whistled softly and stood up. "A real looker. Well, pal, talk to Mary, and I'll see you tomorrow."

"Yeah, tomorrow."

Hank didn't know why he was so uneasy about telling Mary they were moving again. She knew the nature of the business. Hell, she'd probably been expecting it for some time now.

MARY KNEW something was up the minute Hank walked through the front door. She could always tell when he had something heavy on his mind. He was awfully cheerful throughout dinner, but it was forced cheerfulness. He spent a long time with Emily afterward and insisted on supervising her bedtime, even though she was eight and considered herself grown up.

Suddenly it dawned on Mary what was amiss. He hadn't mentioned the business once all evening, and that usually dominated his conversation. *He wants to tell me something,* she thought with insight, *and is dreading it.* After she said good-night to her daughter, she went downstairs and found Hank with his feet propped on an ottoman, reading the newspaper.

"You might as well tell me what's eating you," she said. "It's not going to get any easier."

The paper came down, and Hank slowly shook his head. "You do amaze me, Mary. I've often thought you could read my mind."

"What is it?"

"We're moving."

"I see." Mary's eyes made a brief sweep of the living room. She tried very hard not to get attached to things and to places, but this was such a lovely house, and her garden was the envy of the neighborhood. But in all honesty, she guessed she had seen this coming. Boarded-up buildings were beginning to appear in town, and she'd heard Hank say drilling was down. Several of her friends had moved away during the past year. "Where are we going this time?"

"Farther west. To a place called Rimrock." His eyes brightened, and his words came in a rush as he told her everything Jimmy had said that afternoon. "It's a really huge boom, honey. Maybe the biggest ever."

Where had she heard that before? "When will we be leaving?"

"Well, Jimmy and I are going ahead to scout the area. Then as soon as school is out, you and Emily can join me. Sell the car if you can, and I'll get us a new one in Rimrock."

Mary nodded distractedly. The entire scenario was so achingly familiar. She envied Hank. He could shed belongings the way a bird molts, but it was harder for her. She had been in Ranger six years, a lifetime in the oil business. Emily had friends. She had friends. Store clerks called her by name and held back merchandise they thought she might like. She liked to think she and the other women had done some good for the community.

Impatiently she shook off her thoughts. How stupid to even think about such things! "I'll start getting things ready tomorrow."

Hank stood and went to her, taking her in his arms. "Thanks for taking it so good, honey. I swear I love you more with every passing year."

"And I love you, too, Hank." *I'd have to,* she thought, *to put up with this insane life.* She kissed him lovingly and stood in the warm circle of his arms. What did it matter where they lived as long as they were together?

CHAPTER NINE

Rimrock marked a turning point in my grandparents' lives. That town changed Hank as nothing else ever did, at least for a while. The boom there was twice as big and wild as the one in Ranger had been, but this time Grandpa arrived in town with a fat wallet and plenty of connections. As a full-fledged oilman, he was courted by bankers and the town's businessmen, and he discovered that having money was fun, that he liked being the kind of man others called "sir." He soon abandoned his trademark khakis in favor of store-bought "city clothes." He drank the most expensive liquor he could obtain from a local bootlegger. He passed out dollar tips to waitresses, his barber and the shoeshine boy at the hotel. The one thing he refused to do until his dying day was smoke manufactured cigarettes.

And Mary? Well, she was baffled and sometimes appalled by the changes in a man she thought she knew so well. However, in

typical Mary fashion, she adjusted, coped and
tried to bring normalcy to their lives.

But I'm getting ahead of my story. When
Hank and Jimmy stepped off the T & P at the
Rimrock station, Grandpa was the same old
Hank Travis....

THERE WAS something different about this boom,
Hank thought as he and Jimmy made their way
from the depot to the Pendleton Hotel, though to
the naked eye there didn't seem to be much difference. All the hallmarks of a wide-open oil town
were in place. There were cots lining the alleys, advertised for fifty cents a night. There were the tents
and hastily erected shacks, gin mills and fleshpots
common to all booms. The streets were incredibly
busy, filled with automobiles and buggies of every
description. What once had been a vacant arid
wasteland was now a populated arid wasteland.

Yet for all that, Rimrock had more of a look of
permanence to it than the other places he'd been, as
if it might be around for a long time. Hank knew it
had become a major cattle-shipping center after the
T & P arrived, so the community had a solid eco-
nomic base before oil was discovered. There were a
lot of brick buildings in the main part of town—a
courthouse, two banks, several cafés and drug-
stores, as well as a moving-picture theater. Jimmy
had told him the Permian Basin would pump oil

into the twenty-first century. Hank thought his friend might be exaggerating a tad, but he knew one thing: far West Texas was the place for an oilman to be in. The old rush of excitement stirred in him, as it had during the early days in Ranger.

The Pendleton Hotel's lobby was crowded with its usual patrons—lease hounds, old-time cattle barons and newly rich oilmen. The furniture was heavy and upholstered in well-worn leather. Steer heads decorated the walls, and the air smelled of stale tobacco. Hank and Jimmy registered and sent their luggage up with a bellhop. "Let's go into the coffee shop and have lunch," Jimmy suggested. "I'm starved."

They found a table in front of a window, placed their order and had settled down to survey the local scene when a voice called out.

"Hank Travis! Is that really you, ol' buddy?"

Hank's head swiveled around, and he saw Garmon Holt bearing down on him, hand outstretched. Stifling a groan, he got to his feet and offered his own.

"Hello, Garmon. How's the world treatin' you?"

"Couldn't be better. Hiya, Jimmy. Mind if I sit down? I've been keeping my eyes open, hoping I'd run into you. I've got a sweetheart of a deal for the two of you."

"Have a seat," Hank said. "If it's such a sweet-heart of a deal, why doesn't your old man have it?"

Both men sat down. "Says it's too small. Swear to God, Daddy's gotten to where he thinks he's friggin' Standard Oil or something."

"So what have you got?" Jimmy wanted to know.

"Three-and-a-half sections next door to a big oil field. You know what they say—to find oil, get close to it." Garmon smiled, apparently pleased with himself.

"I know what they say." Jimmy and Hank exchanged amused glances.

"Interested?"

"Maybe," Hank said. "Our company's head geologist here would have to study the deal."

"Of course, of course. Tell you what. The wife and I are having some people over for drinks tonight. You boys come, too. I want you to meet my wife, Hank, and then we can do some talking about this."

Hank looked at Jimmy, who shrugged and nodded his okay. "We'll be there," Hank promised. Frankly, he was dying to get a look at the woman who'd decided to marry Garmon.

"We're at 1104 Van Buren. Six o'clock. Boys, it'd just tickle me to death to have Travis-Blue drill those sections."

"Why?" Jimmy asked.

"For old times' sake, of course. And to see the look on Daddy's face when we hit on a deal that was practically handed to him on a silver platter." Garmon stood. "See you fellows tonight."

After he left, Jimmy looked at Hank. "What's your hunch about that?"

"To be damn suspicious of anything Garmon's doin' on his own, that's what. And I'm not at all sure I want to be in a close business relationship with him, if you know what I mean."

"Yeah, I know what you mean. Still, three-and-a-half sections..."

AFTER LUNCH, Hank found an automobile dealership near the hotel and bought a new Packard. He and Jimmy needed transportation, and the car was guaranteed to make Mary's eyes pop out. She was still in love with the internal combustion engine, and Hank could just picture her sailing around town in the spiffy machine.

Then he and Jimmy spent hours checking out the territory before returning to the hotel to change for the visit with Garmon Holt.

Garmon's house on Van Buren Street was a two-story brick Tudor that looked as though it had twelve acres of front lawn. Moreover, it stood on a street of similarly imposing houses, so Hank assumed that this was where the old cattle barons of the territory had built their homes. It was odd to see a boomtown that could boast of such a high-class neighborhood, and the sight reinforced his belief that Rimrock was a different kind of boom.

A maid opened the door and ushered him and Jimmy inside. "A few people for drinks" turned out to be a mob scene of some fifty or sixty. A glance around convinced Hank that this was a well-heeled crowd. Jimmy soon fell into conversation with two men he had met during his earlier visit to Rimrock, but Hank, of course, didn't know a soul in the place. He was uncomfortable, partly from feeling out of place, partly from being so unaccustomed to a suit and tie. However, he was relieved he had decided to wear them, for every other man there was similarly dressed. Bless Mary for insisting he at least own a suit, even if he'd never before put the thing on.

Someone handed him a drink, which at least gave him something to do with his hands. He tried to concentrate on Jimmy's conversation, but it was all geologists' talk and hard to follow, so he sipped as he wandered through the crowd, and tried to look as if he weren't the outsider he truly was.

The liquor flowed freely—apparently Prohibition didn't exist this far west—and the crowd was loud. It amazed Hank to see so many women participating in the festivities. A good number of them smoked cigarettes, and most of them wore the new short skirts and bobbed hair. The skirts could have gotten them arrested not so long ago. Even Mary had raised her hemlines, declaring that short skirts felt free and disburdening. Hank guessed he was old-fashioned. It just didn't seem right for ladies to show so much leg.

Then Garmon came up behind him. "Hank, ol' buddy, you just gotta meet my wife. Honey, this man and I worked together in Ranger."

Hank smiled, then did a double take and almost choked on his drink. Mrs. Garmon Holt was none other than Billie Jean Surratt. He recognized her immediately, and felt an odd prickling sensation at his nape. Billie Jean!

"Hank!" she screeched.

"You two know each other?" Garmon asked in surprise.

"We went to high school together." Billie Jean then proceeded to plant a kiss on the startled Hank's mouth.

"H-hello, Billie Jean," he managed to stammer. She was just as blonde and curvaceous and pretty as ever, dressed in a skinny little black dress that showed an astonishing amount of skin. She'd always had a gaggle of adoring boys following her around, and for a time he'd been the worst of the lot. He had vaguely pictured her married to some big shot and living in Dallas or Houston. Yet she'd married that ass Garmon of all people! What on earth had she ever seen in him?

But then, maybe the Holt millions could make even Garmon attractive.

"Well, isn't this great!" Garmon gushed enthusiastically. "I'll leave you two to talk old times. I need me a drink." He strolled off.

"My goodness, you're looking good, Hank!" Billie Jean began, her eyes raking him from head to toe. "It's been . . . how many years?"

"Eleven."

"You remember exactly?"

"I remember when I left home. How are your folks?" he asked, in a tone that wasn't entirely polite.

"Fine. They'll be happy to know I've seen you."

"I doubt that."

Billie Jean shot him an offended look that pleased him enormously. "As a matter of fact, they're going to be paying me a visit later on this month," she said. "I want to be sure they see you."

"I wouldn't miss it. How was Europe?"

"Oh, absolutely marvelous, but I swear to goodness, I hope I never see an old castle or museum again."

"This is a pretty nice castle you have here."

"I suppose it is," Billie Jean said disinterestedly. "Here, let me get you another drink. I need one, too. Then we'll go out on the terrace and just talk and talk. My goodness, this is exciting! Seeing you again after all these years and knowing how well you've done."

"How do you know what I've done?"

"Garmon told me he was having the owners of Travis-Blue Production and Exploration over tonight. He made it sound like a very important company. Since I've already met Jimmy Blue, and since you came with him tonight, I have to assume you're the Travis part. Oh, Hank, it's the best news I could have. I worried to death about you after I heard you'd just up and left home for parts unknown."

"Did you now?" Hank was surprised that merely seeing her again had him feeling so malicious.

Billie Jean's chin came up. "Yes, I did. Believe what you choose. Times were different then. I was very young and unsure about the future. I really didn't know what I wanted, and goodness knows, you were...unsettled."

Meaning poor, Hank thought. He shrugged that off and followed her to the bar. "This is quite a party. Do you entertain like this often?"

"Almost every night, it seems. What else is there to do in a burg like Rimrock?"

"How did you meet Garmon?"

"Daddy invested in some of Holt's wells. He introduced us. He and Mama were quite taken with him."

"I'll bet."

Billie Jean bristled slightly. She mixed two drinks and handed one to him. "There you go. Now let's get out of here. The air is stifling."

"AM I TO ASSUME that tonight is not the first time you've seen Mrs. Garmon Holt?" Jimmy asked many hours later as he and Hank drove back to the hotel.

"That's correct. Billie Jean Holt, née Surratt. We met in another lifetime, it seems. We grew up in the same town. She was a doctor's daughter, and I was the son of a peanut farmer."

A few seconds of silence ensued before Jimmy said, "I don't suppose you have to be a world-renowned novelist to come up with the story behind *that*. Did you ever get a chance to talk to Garmon about the deal?"

Hank shook his head. "He was too drunk to talk about anything."

"Yeah," Jimmy said with a nod of his head. "Garmon always did have a particular fondness for joy water."

"Besides, I've decided I don't want to have anything to do with a deal that involves Garmon."

"Hell, this is West Texas, Hank. We ought to at least look at it."

"No," he growled. "We'll find our own deals. First, we need an office, a secretary and a book-keeper. Then I'm gonna find Mary a house."

"Not such a good idea, my man," Jimmy cautioned. "Women like to pick out their own houses."

"She'll like this one because it's gonna be too grand not to like. It's occurred to me that I've kept some of my old peanut-patch mentality when it comes to money. What's the use of havin' the stuff if you don't spend it?"

"When did this revelation come to you? Couldn't have been after finding out the little gal who spurned you once is now married to Garmon Holt, could it? Am I getting warm?"

Hank scowled. "She and that mother of hers always were snobs, and they don't have a tenth of Mary's class. Did you get a good look at those women there tonight? In a real city they'd be treated like sharecroppers, but in Rimrock they're what passes for high society. Well, wait until they meet Mary. Once she becomes mistress of some fine manor, all those women there tonight are gonna be kowtowin' to her like she was the Queen of Sheba or something. Yeah, it won't be long before all those rich bitches are gonna be eatin' out of her hand."

Jimmy uttered a long sigh. "I sure don't like the sound of this."

THE DAY AFTER the party at Garmon's, Hank and Jimmy found a vacant office on Grant Avenue, the town's main street, and two days later they had hired a secretary and a bookkeeper, in the person of Eve Morgan. A graduate of business college, she was a widow with two children in elementary school. Her mother helped out with baby-sitting. Eve was, in fact, too good to be true, and soon proved herself invaluable to Travis-Blue Exploration. From the first day, she ran the office so efficiently that Hank and Jimmy were left free to do other things.

One of Hank's first tasks was to buy a house, and not just an ordinary house, either. When Jimmy saw the place Hank had chosen, he almost choked.

The house was on the east side of town, one street away from the Holt house on Van Buren. It stood back from the street some distance, behind a curved driveway that sliced through what Jimmy supposed would have to be called "grounds." Certainly "lawn" didn't seem adequate. The house itself was an antebellum-cum-Mediterranean castle, dazzling white with plenty of grillwork, and its interior was every bit as opulent as its exterior promised.

"It's something, isn't it?" Hank said proudly.

"That it is," Jimmy agreed. "Who built this place?"

"Some big shot with the T & P. He moved to California."

"The old boy must have had more money than sense."

Hank frowned. "What's the matter with this house?"

"Nothing."

"Yeah, there is. What don't you like?"

Jimmy sighed. "Hank, ol' pal, it's not that I don't like something about the house. But...oilmen are getting the reputation of being free-spending fools as it is, and something like this—" he waved his arm to indicate the house as a whole "—just reinforces that feeling."

"I don't give a damn!" Hank exclaimed. "I worked hard for my money, and I'll spend it on any goddamn thing I like."

"The problem is...every time the boys in Washington get wind of something like this house, they start talking about regulating our industry. Now, I'm not sure what form government regulation would take, but I'll bet my next royalty check that it won't be something we like. It just seems to me it would be better if we all low-keyed things a bit."

"The hell I will!" Hank rolled a cigarette, lit it and inhaled deeply. He stood in the middle of the tiled foyer, his eyes taking in the parlor on the left, the formal dining room on the right, the sweeping staircase ahead. "Who would ever have thought a South Texas peanut farmer's kid would ever own something like this?'' He straightened and looked at Jimmy through a cloud of cigarette smoke. "The woman who sold me this place gave me the name of a decorator in Lubbock. Says he's done a bunch of these houses. Tomorrow I'm gonna get in touch with him and get him started on this place.''

Jimmy's eyes widened. "Hey, a house is one thing, but you can't have someone else decorating the place where Mary's going to live.''

Hank frowned. "I don't have time to wait for Mary to do it.''

''What's the confounded hurry?''

''I'm gonna throw a little party in a few weeks, and I want to be able to show off a little.''

"A party? What in hell for?''

''Officially it's to welcome Mary to Rimrock.''

"And actually?''

''There are some folks comin' to town, and I want to make damn sure they see this place.''

Jimmy sighed but said nothing.

''And that reminds me—I gotta send her a wire right away. She said when she hears from me it'll take her a spell to be ready to leave, and I want her here no later than two weeks from today.''

"So she won't miss the party?''

''Yeah. Come on, let's go.''

At the front door, Hank paused to once again look around. He could hardly wait to see the expressions on the faces of Dr. and Mrs. Surratt when they saw how well the peanut farmer's son had done. A rather unpleasant smile curved his mouth as he closed the door behind him.

"Garmon's asked us over tonight," he told Jimmy. "Wanna go?"

Jimmy shook his head, then shot Hank a suspicious glance. "Are you going?"

"I thought I might. Not much else to do."

"You'd better watch it, Hank. You've been spending a lot of time there."

"Now what in hell is that supposed to mean?"

"Just what I said. Watch it."

"You're talking about Billie Jean," Hank said matter-of-factly.

"It's occurred to me she could get you in a lot of trouble. She has predatory eyes, and it doesn't take a genius to see she can barely stand Garmon."

"Well, you can stop worrying, Jimmy. I'm not about to put my marriage on the line for the likes of Billie Jean Holt. But revenge is sweet. Let me enjoy it."

THAT NIGHT, Hank sat on the sofa in the cavernous living room of Garmon Holt's house, sipping whiskey and water and surveying the unfolding scene. The rooms were packed with people, the same faces he always saw at these gatherings. He sometimes wondered why he bothered attending them. They weren't at all entertaining, but unlike

Jimmy, he couldn't spend night after night in a hotel room with his nose stuck in a book.

"Hank, honey, you don't seem to be having a good time." Billy Jean slid next to him on the sofa.

"Oh... I have a lot on my mind," he hedged.

Billie Jean's mouth formed a pretty pout, the same one she'd used in high school. "I know you must get just as lonely as can be. So do I, believe it or not. Maybe you and I could get together for lunch... or something."

"I'm married."

"Well, shoot, so am I." She giggled.

"I imagine Garmon would take a damn dim view of us having lunch together."

Billie Jean scoffed. "Garmon doesn't know what's going on most of the time. I could have lunch with President Coolidge, and Garmon wouldn't be apt to notice."

"Well, Mary sure would, and she wouldn't like it a bit. Thanks for the invitation, but I'm afraid I'm going to have to pass."

Billie Jean's pout turned into a tight, pinched line. "I know why you're doing this, Hank."

"Oh? Why?"

She studied her manicured nails a second before answering. "To get back at me for all those years ago, when you were willing to work your tail off to give me all the good things in life." She sighed.

"How was I to know then that you'd really be able to do it one day?"

Hank smiled nastily, finished his drink and stood. "You're wrong about my reason, Billie Jean. I'm not having lunch or . . . er, something with you because I'm married to a woman I love very much. Now I think I'm going to call it an evening. Tell Garmon thanks for the drink."

He walked off, leaving his hostess glaring at his retreating figure.

TWO WEEKS LATER, Mary and Emily boarded the T & P for the trip across the vast reaches of West Texas. With each passing mile, Mary's spirits sunk lower and lower. She had never seen such flat, desolate country, and she knew exactly what she would find at their destination—yet another ugly, violent boomtown. The thought was depressing, but living in boomtowns was the only way she could be with Hank.

It had been much harder to leave Ranger than Mary had expected it to be. Friends had called on her every day the past week. She really hadn't realized how many she'd had. Nor had she realized how fond she'd grown of her house. When she'd walked through its rooms for the last time, she had felt a catch in her throat.

In the seat beside her, Emily slept peacefully. She was eight years old now and a joy to be with. Mary had naturally expected there to be more children by now, at least one, but it simply hadn't happened. As it was, mother and daughter had forged a close relationship, perhaps because so often it was just the two of them. In September Emily would be going into the third grade, and Mary did so hope a place called Rimrock would have decent schools. If not, she might have to entertain the painful notion of sending her daughter to a good boarding school.

The miles rolled by; at last the conductor walked through the car calling, "Rimrock next stop."

Mary roused Emily and began gathering up their belongings as the train went whistling and clanging into the station. As the two of them stepped off the train onto the platform, Mary spotted Hank waiting two cars back. She called and waved, and he came running.

"God, I've missed the two of you!" he exclaimed, winding an arm around each of them.

"And we've missed you, Hank," Mary said. Her eyes raked him from head to foot. "You bought a new suit!"

"I bought several new suits."

"Hello, Daddy. Can I have a puppy?"

"A puppy?" Hank asked, as though he'd never heard of such a thing.

"It's all she's talked about," Mary explained. "So many of her friends have pets."

"Then you'll have one, too," Hank promised, giving the child a squeeze. "Come on, I have some real surprises for the two of you."

After gathering together their luggage, Hank led them to the Packard parked in front of the station. "Oh, Hank!" Mary gasped when he informed her it was their new car. "It's magnificent!"

"You haven't seen anything yet. Wait until you get a look at our house." He was grinning from ear to ear.

"You've already found us a house?" House-hunting was usually the first order of business for her.

"Sure have."

"How wonderful!" At least she was spared that chore.

"Let's go, ladies."

Mary took careful notice of this new town. The area near the depot was heavily congested and looked much the way Ranger had the first time she'd seen it. But as they drove farther and farther away from it, the town's appearance slowly changed. She spotted a brick schoolhouse, then street after street of neat frame houses with well-tended yards. Alive with anticipation, she fully expected Hank to stop in front of one of them, but he kept driving.

The houses gradually became bigger and more imposing. Mary saw several that reminded her of the house in Ranger, raising her hopes. Finally, Hank turned onto a street where the houses could only be called mansions. They leaned heavily toward the Southern-plantation style of architecture. Hank pulled into the driveway of one of them.

"Welcome home, honey."

Mary gaped at the house. "Th-this is . . . ours?"

"What do you think?"

"Well . . . what *can* I think? It's so . . . beautiful. I'm just so . . . overwhelmed."

"Go in and have a look around."

Clutching Emily's hand tightly, Mary allowed herself to be taken on a grand tour. As they stepped into the huge foyer, she directed her eyes to the mahogany-railed stairway that swept to the second floor. Hank proudly escorted her in and out of rooms, throwing open closet doors for her inspection. She noticed that the crates she had shipped ahead had not been unpacked—her job, she guessed. But not much from the house in Ranger really seemed appropriate for this one. Some of the bedrooms had been furnished, as had the room Hank referred to as the study. The house had three bathrooms, an unheard-of luxury. It was the grandest, most elegant house she could ever imagine. She was sure she hadn't seen anything in the moving pictures to equal it.

And it was the last house on earth she herself would have chosen.

In the kitchen she was introduced to Lucille, who was the cook. Upstairs she met Elizabeth and Katherine, sisters, who were the maids. Then, from out of the blue, she was accosted by a tall, dapper gentlemen with graying hair and an expansive, eager smile.

"Honey," Hank said, "this is Anthony. He's the decorator of this little ol' place."

Anthony executed a bow. "Mrs. Travis, how wonderful to meet you at last. As soon as you feel rested enough, we'll go over my drawings and samples. It is going to be such a pleasure working with you on this beautiful house."

"Th-thank you," Mary stammered. Then she glanced down at Emily, whose eyes were agog.

"Mama, is this the biggest house in the whole world?"

"It just might be, darling. It just might."

Hank laughed delightedly and draped his arm around Mary's shoulders. "Didn't I once tell you that you belonged in a house like this?"

Mary smiled. "That you did, and you've sure given me one." He looked so pleased with himself. She wouldn't have dreamed of telling him she would have been happier with a house more like the one in Ranger, or with a husband who still wore khakis and disdained the outward trappings of wealth.

Almost immediately, however, she chastised herself. What had happened to her spirit of adventure? "I can hardly wait for Mama to see this place. Duncan, too."

LATER, after Anthony had gone and while Emily was unpacking some of her things and placing them in the bedroom Hank had told her was hers, Mary and Hank sat in the study and talked.

"Well, whad'ya think, honey? Is this house something?"

"Yes, Hank, it's really something...but very unlike you."

He frowned. "In what way?"

"You've always been so careful with money. This house must cost a fortune."

"It's only money. I'm a millionaire now, and it's time I started living like one. You, too."

"How do you figure that?" Mary asked. "How did you come up with that amount?"

"Damn it," he sputtered, quickly growing annoyed. "When you add up all the money I've got in the bank, my oil reserves in the ground, all the equipment I own, you damn well come up with a million dollars!"

Mary was smart enough to know that being worth a million and actually coming up with that amount of cash were two different things entirely. And since when had being a millionaire become important to him? It had never seemed to her that Hank cared all that much about money. "Well . . . it's going to be quite a job just furnishing this place," she said lamely.

"Listen, honey . . . I'd kinda like it if you and Anthony could move pretty fast on this."

Mary frowned. "Why? A house like this takes time."

"Well, I want us to give a big party pretty soon."

"Party? When?"

"Next week."

Mary was certain he was joking. "Hank! I can't possibly have this house ready for guests next week."

"I'd sure appreciate it if you'd try," he said in a surprisingly harsh tone.

Mary looked at him with a start. He'd never spoken to her like that. What was going on? "It's that important?" she asked rather testily.

"Yes."

"Business?"

"You could say that, yes."

Mary was very intuitive when it came to her husband, and she sensed that something complicated was kicking around in that head of his. What it could be she couldn't begin to imagine. "All right," she said coolly. "I'll do my best. But right now, I think I'm going to start moving in. All my clothes will need pressing, and—"

"Mary, honey . . ." Hank's voice detained her.

"Yes."

"There's a place downtown called Tucker's. It's really a nice store. Al Tucker carries big-city things. I've opened a charge account there. You might want to get yourself some fancy duds. Money's no object."

Mary took that as a hint.

WORKING FEVERISHLY, Mary and Anthony got the downstairs rooms done in time for Hank's party. Moreover, she got herself ready, too, by spending an afternoon at Tucker's Department Store. By this time Mary was comfortable with the new styles—short skirts, dropped waists, silk stockings and patent leather shoes. She had become proficient at shaving her legs after many, many nicks and scrapes. The one thing she couldn't bring herself to do was bob her hair. Instead, she waved it around her face, then pulled it into a tight bun at her nape, giving her the appearance of having short hair, at least from the front.

Mary knew she should be having the time of her life. How many women ever got to go on a clothes-shopping binge and decorate a grand house with money no object? Instead she was troubled and had been since her first day in Rimrock. It was a vague something, not as easily identifiable as anger or sorrow or worry, just a feeling that something wasn't quite right in her world. She told herself she was being ridiculous, but the feeling persisted. She would just be glad when Hank's silly party was history. Then perhaps she could shake the notion that she was going to be placed under a microscope, and expected to measure up to...well, to what, she didn't know.

THE DAY OF THE PARTY dawned clear and bright, with just a touch of fall in the air. As usual, Mary got up early in order to get Emily started for the day, though Hank had told her over and over that she was a lady of leisure now, that Elizabeth and Katherine and Lucille would see to Emily first thing every morning.

"That just wouldn't seem right to me," Mary told him.

"Guess it's gonna take you some time to learn to be a rich man's wife."

"Didn't take me any time at all to learn to be Hank Travis's wife." She sniffed. "I'm not too sure I wouldn't prefer just being that and not having to pretend to be something I'm not."

"The two of us have a lot to learn about playing in the big time, honey."

"I really don't much like the idea of being in the big time, Hank."

"Well, I don't guess it much matters, Mary, because we're sure there."

That was the end of the discussion, and Mary tried not to bring it up again.

She expected to have dozens of last-minute things to do that day, but once Hank had left for the office and Emily was at play, she discovered there was absolutely nothing for her to do. The house was as clean as human hands could make it, thanks to Katherine and Elizabeth. Lucille had the food and drink department firmly in control, and the last thing she wanted was "help" from the lady of the house. Finally, after a solitary lunch, Mary carried some magazines upstairs and read them, listening to the muted sounds of the household below. Girlish squeals wafted through the open window from the backyard below. In the resourceful way of children, Emily had promptly gone out and found a girl her age who lived four doors down. *It would be nice,* Mary thought, *if I could just prowl the neighborhood until I saw a friendly face.*

Giving a growl of self-disgust, she threw down the magazine she was reading and stood up. No doubt she would meet a lot of friendly faces tonight, some of whom would be her new friends. Tonight was important to Hank, so it was going to be important to her, too. She didn't know what was wrong with her. She hated thinking she was getting overly touchy and sensitive where her husband was concerned. Or worse, that she had forgotten how to live her own life.

Crossing the room, she flung open the door to her closet, a closet that was the size of a small sitting room. Hank had a similar one across the room.

Hers was filled with clothes, most of them new, as Hank wished. He wanted her to knock everyone's eyes out tonight, so she was going to do her best.

Her eyes fell on one particular garment, the most expensive she had purchased. It was made of rose silk crepe and was exquisite in every soft, clinging detail. It had a scooped neckline, dropped waist banded in silk, and its hem came just below the knee. The saleslady at Tucker's had declared that it epitomized the French influence on American fashion. Mary knew next to nothing about high fashion, but the dress was beautiful. Smiling, she closed the door. If clothes could do it, that dress should.

MARY'S EFFORTS were rewarded some hours later when Hank came out of his dressing room, fresh from his shower and wrapped in a towel, and beheld her in her finery. He stopped and uttered a low whistle. "Mary, honey, you look absolutely beautiful!"

She executed a little pirouette. "Like it?"

"I love it."

"Is this what you had in mind?"

"Exactly. Hot damn, I'm gonna be the envy of every man here tonight." Dropping his towel, he went into his closet to begin getting dressed.

"Why is that important to you?"

Hank looked over his shoulder with a frown. "Why? 'Cause every man likes thinkin' he's got the best-lookin' wife in the whole world, that's why."

Mary sat on the chaise, crossed her legs, locking her hands around one knee, and watched him. Hank would never be a large man, but he was a magnificent specimen, strong and muscular. He would turn thirty on his next birthday, a prime bull at the height of his powers. Mary was enormously proud of all he had accomplished when he had started out with so little. But she wasn't happy over the change in his attitude toward having money. It was very un-Hank-like, to her notion.

Mary heard the sound of the doorbell and gave a start. "Will that be the first of the guests?" she asked anxiously.

"Probably."

"Shouldn't we be downstairs to greet them?

"Jimmy'll do it. We'll make our grand entrance in a little bit."

Just thinking about walking down that imposing stairway with all eyes trained on her started butterflies flitting in Mary's stomach, but she said nothing. Tonight they would do things Hank's way. Depending on how things went, she might have to have a talk with him tomorrow.

"What's Emily doing tonight?" Hank asked.

"After supper, she's going to Lucille's room to learn to play mah-jongg."

"What in hell's that?"

"Some kind of game that's all the rage. I must say that Emily seems to have acquired three devoted servants in Lucille, Elizabeth and Katherine. I wonder if that's wise. I don't want her getting spoiled."

"Don't worry about the scamp, honey. She's a good kid." Hank finished dressing and gave himself one last inspection in the mirror. Mary thought he looked marvelous in his dark suit, white shirt and subdued tie—the absolute picture of success. He certainly didn't much resemble that frail boy she'd first seen at YH Ranch. Sometimes when she studied her husband, her heart would seem to swell to twice its normal size. She so hoped Rimrock wouldn't ruin him, then wondered why she even thought it might.

Apparently Hank himself was satisfied with his appearance. Slicking back his hair one more time, he straightened his tie, then formed an exaggerated crook with his elbow.

"Come on, honey, let's go give the riffraff a thrill."

"Oh, Hank," Mary said in barely disguised dismay. "What an attitude!"

"I want you to remember something tonight," he said, wagging a finger for emphasis. "Just remember that you can buy and sell anyone here any day of the week. And don't ever forget it. Let's go."

CHAPTER TEN

THE DISTANCE from the second floor landing to the foyer seemed like a yawning mile to Mary. She and Hank slowly began their descent, and as she'd feared, all eyes turned upward. She quickly discovered something about herself at that moment: she didn't enjoy being the center of attention. She would have wagered Hank felt the same way, but right now he seemed to be having a wonderful time.

"Ah, there are our hosts," a booming masculine voice exclaimed, and Mary saw a well-dressed, portly man with salt-and-pepper hair advancing on them.

"Honey," Hank said, "this is R. G. Gregson. He's the president of First State Bank. R.G., this is my wife, Mary."

R.G. took both her hands between his. "How nice to meet you at last, my dear. This is my wife, Kitty."

Kitty was a round, dimpled blonde with a Clara Bow mouth, the kind men of all ages probably found irresistible. She was dressed in brilliant red and would have stood out in a crowd of five hundred. "Oh, Mary, I'm so glad to meet you!" Kitty shrieked. "You'll be such a refreshing addition to our little circle. Do you play bridge?"

"No, I..."

"Well, you'll have to learn. What would our days be without bridge? And once you and Hank join the country club, you'll be able to enjoy our luncheons and teas...not to mention the cocktail hour. Oh, the club does do such wonderful little tidbits. And Sunday night supper at the club is a must. We're not Dallas or Fort Worth, by any means, but we do try to bring a little refinement to the backwater." Kitty's head swiveled around. "Tessie! *Tess-eee!* Come over here and meet Mary!" Turning back to Mary, Kitty confided, "Tessie's my best friend. You'll love her."

A large, rather lumpy woman with a shocking mass of red hair lumbered over to them. Tessie was the very picture of an inelegant farm girl dressed in her Sunday best. That she and Kitty could be best friends amazed Mary, but she decided the marked difference between them was probably what drew them together.

"Tessie," Kitty said, "*this* is Mary."

"Well, ain't you a pretty little thing!" Tessie exclaimed in a husky voice.

"Thank you, Tessie. It's so nice to meet you."

"Mary doesn't play bridge," Kitty said to her friend. "I told her she simply must learn."

"Oh, Gawd, yes!" Tessie replied. "It's the only way to get acquainted."

The thought of spending her days at a bridge table or the country club depressed Mary to no end.

Suddenly Hank, who had been in conversation with R.G., seized her arm. "Sorry, ladies, but Mary has a lot of people to meet tonight. I'm gonna have to spirit her away."

"I'll get with you later, Mary," Kitty promised, and she and Tessie headed toward the lavish buffet that had been set up in the dining room.

"Here you go, honey," Hank said, gesturing toward an immaculately clad middle-aged couple standing apart from the crowd. "I especially want you to meet these folks."

Mary had a brief second to study the couple before Hank thrust her in front of them. They were probably in their fifties, very well-preserved fifties at that. They somehow exuded breeding and money, like some of the parents of her fellow students at Mayberry Academy. She glanced sideways at Hank. The look on his face was one of pure triumph. *Who are these people and what do they mean to my husband?*

"Mrs. Surratt. Dr. Surratt," Hank said formally.

The woman stepped forward and grabbed Hank's hand. "Oh, Hank, I can't tell you...I mean, when Billie Jean told us who owned this beautiful house...well, we were so..."

"Surprised?" he asked.

"Well, yes...and thrilled for you, of course."

"Quite a step up in the world for a peanut farmer's son, right?"

Mary shot Hank a peculiar look. His voice had a nasty edge to it, and she thought the remark had been rude and uncalled for. *What in the world is wrong with him tonight?* The smile on Mrs. Surratt's face froze. Nervously, the woman reached for her husband's hand. "You remember my husband, I'm sure."

"Oh, yes," Hank said, extending his hand. "How are you, Doctor?"

"Fine, fine. It's nice to see you, Hank."

"And I want both of you to meet my wife. This is Mary."

He stepped back and nudged Mary in front of him. She felt as though she were on display, like a prize heifer. She sensed that a great deal was expected of her. Unfortunately, she didn't know what it was. The Surratts did not openly stare at her—they were much too well-bred for that—but they scrutinized her as thoroughly as politeness would allow. For Mary it was a stunning experience.

Introductions were acknowledged and pleasantries exchanged. Then they were joined by another couple, who were introduced to Mary as Garmon and Billie Jean Holt. Billie Jean, she learned, was the Surratts' daughter.

"Oh, you're Mary!" Billie Jean exclaimed. "How wonderful to meet you at last. Hank's told me so much about you. We must get together soon."

Garmon was already well on his way to being drunk. "Hank, ol' buddy, you son of a gun...you really know how to pick 'em. I tell you, Mary...this husband of yours...well, he was such a good ol' buddy...I mean, this man and I..."

Mary saw Billie Jean roll her eyes in disgust. But she covered it quickly, took Mary by the arm and led her away. "I hope this mob scene doesn't frighten you to death," she said in a confidential manner. "I don't know half these people, and I thought I knew everyone in this dreadful town. I'll bet Hank doesn't know them, either."

"Have you known my husband long, Billie Jean?" Mary asked, her curiosity about the Surratts soaring off into space.

"Oh, forever! We knew each other in high school."

High school? Mary's mind quickened. Billie Jean's father had been introduced as "Doctor." That would have placed Hank and Billie Jean at opposite ends of the social spectrum in a small South Texas town. Did that have something to do with the way Hank was acting tonight?

"It must have been a surprise to run into him again after so many years," Mary said.

"Oh, it was. He's done well. You must be proud of him."

"I am," Mary said, "but then I was proud of him long before there was a Travis-Blue Production and Exploration Company."

Mary meant that only as a simple statement of fact, but for a fleeting second, Billie Jean seemed to stare daggers at her. Then she smiled sweetly. "Of course."

There was something about Billie Jean Holt that unnerved Mary and made her feel vulnerable, which was pretty ridiculous when she thought about it. She never made snap judgments about people, but she'd already decided Billie Jean was the sort of "friend" one needed to watch carefully. "Have you and your husband been here long?" she asked politely.

"Long enough," Billie Jean answered with a sort of sigh.

"Is this a temporary move or will you be here awhile?"

"Who knows. Whatever Garmon's daddy tells us to do is what we'll do. Come on, Mary, I'll introduce you around, and remember not to take any of these people seriously. There's Billy Hubbard," she said, indicating a smiling bull of a man. "Two years ago he and Tessie were milking cows and slopping hogs. Then my father-in-law found oil on their farm. Now they're filthy rich. But they're still dirt farmers down deep inside. Now those people over there..."

HANK GRABBED Jimmy by the arm and pulled him aside. "How in hell did you get such a crowd together?"

"I invited R. G. Gregson and told him to invite everybody he knows and to tell them to invite everybody *they* know. Quite possibly there are some gate-crashers. This little soiree is going to set you back a pretty penny, pal."

"Who cares? You did good, Jimmy."

"I wish I knew why this nonsense is so important to you," Jimmy grumbled.

MUCH LATER, after the hard-core drinkers had finally left, mercifully enabling the host and hostess to retire upstairs, Mary lay propped in bed, watching her husband undress.

"You're gloating, Hank," she teased. "Positively gloating."

"You know anyone who's got a better right?"

Mary sobered. "I know tonight was meant to prove something."

"I'll tell you what it was meant to prove. That Travis-Blue is no fly-by-night outfit, that we can compete with the biggest. That we have some serious money behind us. That we're not a couple of yokels."

Mary digested that and discovered that it bothered her tremendously. She waited a minute before asking, "Who are the Surratts?"

Hank hesitated a split second before answering. "I knew them back in South Texas."

"I know. Billie Jean told me that much."

"Then why did you ask?"

"I sense they were important to you, that maybe tonight...well, maybe they were the reason for tonight's party."

Hank grunted. "Yeah, they were important to me. They treated me like dirt when I was a kid, but they won't anymore."

Mary knew she couldn't begin to understand that kind of demon. "And that makes you happy?"

"You're damn right. As happy as I can get."

Mary sighed, then shook off her dismay. She patted the pillow and gave him a smile. "Want to bet?"

Hank slid in beside her and turned off the bedside lamp. Her hands fluttered over him. "Well...*almost* as happy as I can get. You were wonderful tonight, honey. Damn, I was proud of you. You really put the rest of the women in the shade.''

Mary ignored that and arched toward him. They moved together slowly, letting their needs smolder. There was no rush, just quiet touching and urging until a subtle shift in rhythm created tiny explosions inside Mary. She had never ceased to be amazed at how attuned their bodies were. They wound themselves around each other and rolled over the bed, length to length. And when at last he slipped into her, filling her, the sensation was as comforting as warmth and light.

But long after Hank was satisfied and asleep, she lay awake. She sensed that this town, this house, all these new people combined to create the first real test of their marriage, and she vowed that the union *would* pass it, no matter what.

HANK HAD ALWAYS THOUGHT he was luckier when Mary was nearby, and the following afternoon proved it. While he and Jimmy were entertaining Eve with reminiscences about other booms they had known, a lease scout walked into the office to offer Travis-Blue four sections in Winston County, south of Rimrock. Over coffee, the broker told the partners he had offered the deal to all the majors and most of the independents and had been turned down by all. Furthermore, there was a dry hole about a mile to the north, and there was no drilling going on anywhere near the lease.

The whole deal sounded so unpromising that Hank couldn't understand the churning in his gut. He told the broker he would think it over, then immediately dispatched Jimmy to Winston County. The next day the geologist came back with an unenthusiastic report.

"It's way outside the play, Hank, and just north is an abandoned field that was drained dry in a year. Of course, a lot of that was pure waste. And that dry hole the broker mentioned was plugged and abandoned because the operator went broke. I talked to an old roustabout who worked on it, and he said they could have made a well if the money hadn't run out."

"So... what are you telling me?" Hank asked.

"Nothing. Just thinking out loud."

Hank tapped on the desktop with a pencil. "God, I've got me a strong feelin' about this deal."

"That's probably as good a thing to go on as anything," Jimmy said lazily.

Hank stewed on it for days, hoping for one of his visions. Finally he drove to Winston County himself and found the lease. He walked through ankle-high prairie grass and scanned a cloudless sky that seemed to go on forever. "Saint Rita!" he called to the heavens. "If you could tell those Yankees where to drill, how about giving *me* a sign? Something.

Anything." But the only sound he heard was the ceaseless wind.

Shoving his hands in his pockets, he kept walking. Finally, he reversed direction and headed for his car. And at that moment, a jackrabbit hopped out of the grass not twenty yards away. Hank smiled. The farmers and ranchers hated the pesky creatures, but they were funny-looking and kind of cute, with their floppy ears and powerful hind legs.

As Hank watched, the animal seemed to stumble, apparently having stepped in a prairie dog hole. It extricated itself quickly, then hopped off, favoring one foot. Hank's eyes widened. Rabbit's foot!

It was all he needed. "Thanks, Rita," he yelled, grinning. "You're a sweetheart!"

Hurrying back to town, he found the broker and grabbed the leases. Travis-Blue's Winston Number One was spudded in within weeks. Two years later, there were producing wells flowing all over the area. Later still, when the great Winston County Field had been defined, Travis-Blue's four sections lay in the heart of it.

Such was the stuff of legends in the West Texas of those days. A lot of people got rich in Winston County—big oilmen and movie stars who didn't need the money, and some little guys who did. But it was Travis-Blue that had drilled the discovery well, and that fact wasn't lost on the worshipers of black gold. Hank and Jimmy acquired the invaluable reputation of being knowledgeable operators, good men to know and to deal with. They also were lucky, which counted for far more than knowledge in the oil patch.

FOR A WOMAN who had always sought out and thrived on challenge, Mary discovered that the early years in Rimrock presented the greatest challenge of all. There were times when they tested her mettle to the limit.

For one thing, she had come to what surely was the wind and dust capital of North America. In spring, when the fallow farms north of the town began to stir, filling the air with yellow-orange grit, she had to stay indoors most of the time. But Mary had never let her rather delicate health indispose her for long. It was, to her, a minor annoyance that she had learned to cope with.

The style of living that Hank had decided to embrace was another matter. It bothered her enormously to live a life that consisted chiefly of rising at her leisure, eating a breakfast that someone else had prepared for her, dressing for the day and then . . . Then what?

Sensing from the beginning that there would be little for her to do, she had dawdled over finishing the decoration of the house, somehow making the project last a year, but one day it was done, with no need for so much as one more knickknack. Then Mary had more time than anything.

But at least her family was busy and happy. Emily was completely caught up with a growing circle of playmates, and she absolutely adored Ralph, the Great Dane her father had bought her. Unlike most children, Emily had never turned Ralph over to the adults when the newness of having him around wore off. She and the dog were constant companions, and she took care of all his needs, from feeding to grooming to accompanying him to the veterinarian.

And Hank? Mary hardly ever saw her husband. Travis-Blue had become a fast-moving operation. While Jimmy ran the office and checked out deals, Hank logged many a rail mile to places like St. Louis and Chicago, where he met with big-city investors who were anxious to profit from Texas oil. He loved every minute of it.

Only Mary was at loose ends. Of course there were plenty of women who tried to take her under their wings. Billie Jean Holt, in particular, seemed to be standing on her doorstep every time she looked up. But Mary always suspected it wasn't Mary Travis who interested Billie Jean half as much as the rags-to-riches aura that surrounded Hank. In fact, she soon realized that none of their new friends led lives of any real significance, that they rushed from party to party as though frightened to death of finding themselves with an idle hour or so. All that money and all that leisure were opiates to which Mary was determined she and Hank would never succumb.

There was something out there that would grab her interest; she was sure of it. All she had to do was wait for it to present itself.

ONE AFTERNOON in late 1925, while she was shopping on Grant Avenue, Mary decided to stop by the office and say hello to Eve Morgan. She found one very busy secretary-bookkeeper who seemed to need another pair of hands.

"End of the month," Eve apologized, brushing her ash-blond hair away from her face. "I've got to get the payroll out or I'll have two dozen roughnecks marching on this office. And the phone has been ringing off the wall."

"Can I give you a hand?" Mary asked. "I can at least answer the phone."

"Would you? What a help! Just tell everyone that Mr. Blue is out of the office until five and Mr. Travis is out of town, then take names and numbers. That'll leave me to concentrate on the payroll."

The afternoon fairly flew by. Mary had always been interested in the business because Hank was so thoroughly involved in it, but after that afternoon she found herself wanting to become active in it.

She waited until the day's activity slowed and it was almost time for Eve to close up the office to bring up the subject.

"Are you serious?" Eve asked in surprise. "I'd love to have you. You were a big help this afternoon, and when things are slow, I'd love having someone to talk to."

"So would I, Eve. Some days I just ramble around that big house. I think I've read more books this past year than I did in all the previous years of my life put together."

Eve eyed Mary speculatively. "Is this crazy life getting you down?"

Mary shrugged and uttered a little laugh. "It shouldn't. I've been in it long enough to have become used to it, God knows, but here in Rimrock... Well, things are different somehow. Here it's just rush, rush, money, money."

"Yeah, I know. I've been around the oil business a long time. My dad worked the rigs and so did my husband. In fact, he got himself killed in a blowout down at Big Lake. I've known a lot of oilers, and I know what the successful ones are like. Like kids in a candy store, that's what. Once they make a lot of money, the world is offered to them, and they find it hard to turn down."

"But Hank was never like that," Mary protested. "Never!"

"A lot of money changes people, more than anything else, I sometimes think. Especially those who started out with nothing. This town is full of overnight millionaires who were all but starving a couple of months ago. Of course, it's also full of overnight paupers who had the world by the tail a couple of months ago. I'm telling you, Mary, risking everything on the turn of a drill bit is crazy, and it takes a certain kind of person to do it."

Someone like my husband, Mary thought. She'd often suspected that had Hank lived in another time and place, he would have been a riverboat gambler. "Eve, you say men like Hank and Jimmy are offered everything. For instance?"

Eve dug around in a desk drawer and came up with some papers. "For instance, stuff like this. Nonsense, I'd call it, but I can't very well say anything. It's certainly not my place to tell Hank and Jimmy what to do with their money."

Maybe not, but Mary figured it *was* her place, and she was aghast at some of the things Hank and Jimmy were considering. She said absolutely no to the company's plans to open another office in Midland or Odessa simply because some of the other independents were doing it. She also vetoed Hank's grand plans to build a guest cottage behind their house, since the place was already too big for their needs. Similarly, she said, no, the company didn't need a private railroad car, not when the

T & P overnight accommodations to Fort Worth and El Paso were luxurious enough for everyone.

Mary doubted either Hank or Jimmy truly appreciated her frugality, but while friends and associates spent money like water, she made sure Travis-Blue didn't. It was largely through her efforts that the company made its way through the dizzying prosperity of the twenties on an even keel, never experiencing the feast-or-famine cycles so common to the oil business. Dry holes and unwanted gas wells were disappointments rather than disasters.

The one person who recognized and applauded Mary's common sense was Eve. Mary had made her first real friend in Rimrock. Eve was straightforward, down-to-earth and shared Mary's passion for the movies, as they were now called. Since she was a widow and Mary felt like one half of the time, the two women tried to get together one night a week for dinner and a movie. And it was chiefly through Mary's efforts that Eve and Jimmy began dating.

Mary had suspected for some time that her friend had a huge crush on Jimmy, and during one of their evenings out, when confronted with the question, Eve admitted it.

"But I might as well have a crush on the filing cabinets. He just looks right through me. It's a very humbling experience, I'll tell you. You don't suppose he's...well, that he doesn't like women, do you?"

Mary gave it some thought. It was possible. She didn't know for sure how old Jimmy was, but he was several years older than Hank, which would put him in his late thirties. And he'd never been married.

"Well," she said, "there's only one way to find out. You're going to have to get a date with him."

"How am I going to do that when he looks right through me?"

"I know! Since Hank is on one of his rare 'visits' home, I'll ask the two of you over for dinner. Then you say something about not having a car, you promised your mother she could use it or something. So I'll ask Jimmy if he would mind picking you up, and being a gentleman, he'll say of course not. After that it's up to you...and to Jimmy."

"You have the mind of a genius," Eve said admiringly. "You don't believe in sitting back and waiting for things to happen, do you?"

"Remind me sometime to tell you how I got Hank to marry me."

MARY PROVED to have great matchmaking skills. That evening's dinner was a resounding success, and Jimmy acted looser and freer that she'd ever seen him. She wasn't at all surprised when he and

Eve began dating steadily or when they married six months later. It was, however, something of a shock to see Jimmy transformed from confirmed bachelor to family man.

"What kind of daddy do you figure you're gonna make?" Hank asked right after the wedding.

"Eve's had 'em alone a long time, and they're good kids. Don't reckon I can mess 'em up too bad."

After that the Travises and the Blues were inseparable, both in business and on the social scene. Mary and Eve ran the office while "the boys" did the legwork. Those were the happiest years of Mary's life. The papers referred to the times as "the era of wonderful nonsense," and it did seem that everyone was a little giddy and silly and heady with success. Making money seemed to be the easiest thing in the world.

The news in 1929 that the stock market had collapsed caused barely a ripple of interest out in the far reaches of West Texas. What did something that happened in the industrial Northeast have to do with the booming oil business? Travis-Blue was successful beyond anyone's wildest dreams, and there wasn't a reason in the world to expect that to change.

CHAPTER ELEVEN

MARY PATIENTLY STRODE up and down the platform outside the T & P depot in Rimrock. The
ticket agent had just changed the message on the
blackboard outside the station. The train from Fort
Worth, it now read, would be twenty-five minutes
late. *A good guess,* she thought. Railroad sched-
ules had always mystified her. To her knowledge,
the five-thirty from Fort Worth had never made
Rimrock before six, so why didn't the agents own
up to it and post that as the arrival time?

Occasionally she paused and squinted down the
tracks, more out of habit than anything. On the flat
prairie, the big locomotive could be seen and heard
long before it came clanging into the station. She
wondered how much time she had spent either
dropping Hank off at the depot or picking him up.
It had become a twice-a-month routine, and they
had been in Rimrock seven years now.

It was October, 1930, and Hank had been away
from home almost a month, an unusually long
time. Normally his trips to St. Louis took no more

than ten days, often less. Though he had called the office several times whenever he was away, Mary never felt satisfied with the few words they exchanged before the phone was given to Jimmy. Long distance calls were expensive and kept as short as possible.

Her intuition had been working overtime lately, and she sensed something was afoot. For one thing, Hank had spent more than a week in Fort Worth on the return journey, something he'd never done. Usually when he started for home, he made no detours, claiming he was like a horse heading for the barn at the end of the day. Mary hoped he had found some promising investors in Fort Worth. If so, his time away from home would be greatly diminished.

She returned to her pacing until the train came whistling into the station. Hank stepped out of the third car back, his suit jacket over one arm. His tie had been loosened, his shirt was open at the neck, and in one hand he carried his ever-present briefcase. A smile wreathed his face when he saw her, and his pace quickened.

Mary watched him, and concern suddenly furrowed her brow. He was almost thirty-seven, and for the first time, he was beginning to look it. There was a bit of softening around the middle, attributable no doubt to all the sippin' whiskey that was consumed while deals were consummated. And the laugh lines around his eyes had deepened; the jaw-line was a bit less firm. Why hadn't she noticed that before? *We don't have all the time in the world anymore!* she thought in dismay. *We need to slow down, take a vacation and start thinking about where we want to be, what we want to be doing ten years from now.*

"Hello, honey," he said, looping an arm around her and planting a warm kiss on her mouth. "How's my girl?"

"A lot better than I was five minutes ago. How was your trip?"

"I'll tell you about it when we get home."

That remark alone told Mary that this trip had somehow been different. Usually he just said, "Great!" and left it at that.

When the porters had unloaded the luggage, Hank retrieved his bag, and they strolled over to the big Lincoln town car parked in front of the depot. "You drive, honey," Hank said. "I'm beat."

Once at the house, they were accosted, first by Ralph and his barking welcome, then by Lucille, who wanted to know when the mister wanted dinner. Hank asked for an hour to relax and have a drink. He could have asked for three or four hours, and it wouldn't have daunted Lucille, who could prepare any amount of food for any number of people on almost no notice.

Then Emily bounded down the stairs, still dressed in the plaid jumper and white blouse she had worn to school that day. At fifteen she was bright and inquisitive, a blossoming beauty who seemed blessed with unlimited energy.

"Hello, Daddy," she said, slipping her arms around him.

"Hello, sweetheart. Anything new in your world?"

"Not really."

"Don't be modest, honey," Mary said. "Tell him."

"Well . . . my American history teacher asked everyone to write a letter to the President, telling him what all we've been studying. Then she'd decide which one to send him. And she picked mine. My letter's being sent to President Hoover."

"That's great, sweetheart," Hank said. "Ol' Herbert could probably use a smile in the day's mail."

"Well, I'm going over to Becky's, Mama. Just call me when it's time to come home."

"All right, honey. It'll be in about an hour."

"Come on, Ralph," Emily said, gesturing to her ever-present pet. "You come along, but you'll have to wait outside."

As Hank headed upstairs, Mary mixed a Scotch and water at the bar. Then she carried it to their bedroom, where Hank was changing.

"You look tired, Hank," she said, perching on the edge of the chaise and studying him intently. "What happened?"

"What makes you think something happened?" he asked as he shrugged out of his dress shirt and reached for the silk robe known as a smoking jacket. He then rolled and lit a cigarette.

"Hank, please... This is me you're talking to."

"I forgot you can read my mind."

"Sometimes I wish I could. But I always know when something's up."

He nudged her over and sat beside her. "The big-city investors are drying up, honey. They've got problems."

Mary frowned. "That stuff that's going on up north?"

Hank nodded. "It's not just up north anymore. The whole country's going to suffer. It's bad, Mary. A lot worse than we thought."

"But... everything here seems so normal. What do we care what happens in the stock market? We don't have any money invested in the thing."

"It's gonna affect us, sooner than we thought. On an impulse, I called Duncan before I left Fort Worth. He asked me to stop and spend the night at the YH, so I did. We had us a real nice visit, but he's worried. He says the price of beef on the hoof has taken a bad dive."

"He's not in serious trouble, is he?" Mary asked with alarm.

"I don't think so, but he's probably got some lean years ahead of him. I'm thinkin'...well, I'm thinkin' we might oughta get out while the gettin's good."

Mary wasn't sure she understood. "Out? Out of what? West Texas, the oil business, what?"

Hank stood and walked to the window, staring out thoughtfully for several silent minutes. Mary studied his back, the old trepidation overtaking her. He was acting exactly the way he had that night in Ranger when he'd told her they were moving to Rimrock, moving on to greater opportunities.

But that had been seven years ago, and Ranger had been a boomtown that was playing out. Rimrock still screamed of opportunity and prosperity. The community's population had doubled every two years or so. It was a busy place where fortunes were made every week, and she and Hank were entrenched as solid citizens. It had, to Mary's own astonishment, become home.

"Hank, why did you stay in Fort Worth so long?" she asked.

He turned and faced her. "I just headquartered in Fort Worth. I spent most of my time in a place called Kilgore."

"Why?"

Hank stubbed out his cigarette in an ashtray and returned to sit beside her. His eyes were alive with excitement. Seeing them, Mary's heart sank. She could predict what was coming.

"Honey, a couple of weeks ago an old man named Joiner brought in a well called the Daisy Bradford. He'd been working on the damn thing for *four* years, and it finally came in. Listen to this. It's flowing *sixty-eight-hundred barrels a day!* It's unbelievable!"

Mary simply stared at him.

Hank didn't notice. He jumped to his feet and paced up and down in front of her. "But that's not the best part. The best part is—the general feeling is that the majority of the oil is east of Joiner's lease. But I went back to the hotel, lay down and had a dream. The mama cat is west of that lease, and it's a pool bigger'n...well, maybe bigger'n Manhattan! Maybe twice as big."

"Oh, Hank." Mary sighed, knowing he didn't have the first idea how big Manhattan was. She never made light of his visions because he had been right so many times, so there probably was a great big oil field over in East Texas. But did that mean he had to go chasing it? What about all they had here?

"I'm tellin' you, honey, it's...it's..."

"The granddaddy of them all?" she suggested a trifle skeptically.

"Yes! Damn right! Nobody has any idea how big it's gonna be."

"So?"

"So I leased everything I could west of the Joiner lease."

Mary's eyes widened. "Does Jimmy know this?"

"He'll find out tomorrow."

"Hank, you have a partner!" Mary exclaimed. "You can't operate independently of Jimmy."

"I didn't have time to wait for Jimmy's go-ahead. People are streaming into the place in droves. You know the picture."

Yes, she knew. She could see it as clearly as if she were there. Another wild, lawless boomtown, awash in mud or dust, where gentility and decency didn't exist. She supposed she would never understand why the quest for black gold turned people so greedy and dangerous.

"So," she said with a sigh, "I assume you have plans to develop those leases. That's going to be hard to do, isn't it? You have so much going on here with the company and all."

"I know. That's . . . er, something else I want to talk to you about. I've had an offer for Travis-Blue."

Mary sat in stunned silence a minute. "Sell the company?" she exclaimed at last.

"It's a good offer from one of the majors. Several million dollars."

"But...what would you do without the company?"

"Start all over again," he said with a smile.

Mary wasn't smiling; she was thunderstruck. "Are you talking about...wildcatting again? On your own?"

He nodded.

A picture was beginning to form in her mind. "Let me get this straight. You want to sell Travis-Blue and light out for this new big boom."

"Yes," Hank said emphatically. "It's exciting, Mary. Just like the old days."

"And I assume you want Emily and me to go with you to...to wherever it is."

"Yes, of course. Remember Ranger? Remember Rimrock when we first got here? There was something new every minute!"

"Yes, I remember," Mary said dully. Her chest rose and fell, and at that moment she accepted as reality something that had only been a question before. Hank would never settle down for long, not until he was too old or too sick to move on. Somewhere on the face of the earth there would always be another boom, and he'd want to be there. That was more enticing to him than great riches. The money had been exciting only while it was new. Now it was old hat.

"No," she said with finality.

Hank's eyes widened. "No?" he asked incredulously.

"No."

"I don't believe it! What happened to that spunky gal who was always out for another adventure?"

She took both his hands in hers and gave them a shake. "Oh, Hank, I'm not eighteen anymore! I'm not going to move to another dirty, wild boomtown. I have a fifteen-year-old daughter to think about. I'm not going to take her to a place like that." Dropping his hands, she clasped hers tightly together. "Now, I'm . . . I'm going downstairs and tell Lucille to start dinner. I'll get you another drink." With that, she turned on her heel and left the room. Hank stared after her in disbelief. He couldn't believe his ears. No? Mary had said no! It was the last thing on earth he had expected. He lit another cigarette and walked to the window, staring down at the grounds below.

So now what did he do? Forget East Texas? Sell those leases, which would bring a damn sight more than he'd paid for them? He smiled ruefully. That was the way he and Jimmy had started. And hadn't it been fun in those days!

That was his problem, he knew. Being a big-shot, millionaire oilman wasn't the fun that scrounging leases and poor-boyin' that first well had been, even if the damn thing had gone up in smoke. He hadn't even realized he was bored until he'd gone to Kilgore and seen the excitement. He wanted to be in on it!

Most of all he didn't want to be one of Rimrock's idle rich. He thought of the people he knew—R.G. and Kitty, Billy and Tessie, Garmon and Billie Jean, and a half dozen other couples just like them. The women gossiped over the bridge table and spent money, while their husbands played golf and poker and spent money. He'd proved himself and no longer wanted to be like them. He wanted to be out with the working stiffs.

Now Mary had taken the wind out of his sails. The longer he thought about it, the madder he got. Damn it, she was his wife, and wives went where their husbands did. And if he missed East Texas, he'd regret it the rest of his life. By the time Mary returned with a fresh drink for him, he was good and steamed.

"Now you listen to me!" he said, pointing his finger at her. "You're my wife, and your place is with me, no matter where it is. Got that?"

Her mouth dropped. Deliberately she set the drink down on the dresser and folded her arms under her breasts. "Stop pointing that finger! And don't you talk to me in that tone of voice!"

Hank grabbed the drink and downed it in two gulps before slamming the glass down on the dresser. "I've given you every goddamn thing in the world, and the thanks I get is having you say no to something you have to know is important to me."

"Yes, you've given me a very nice life. And I've come to like it. And if you don't mind my saying so, I deserve it, goodness knows. That's why I'm not going to another dirty, lawless boomtown. I'm fed up with places like that. They aren't even civilized."

Hank stared at her a minute. Then he took off the smoking jacket and reached for the shirt he'd worn earlier. "Count me out for dinner."

"Where are you going?"

"I'm going to see Jimmy." He was halfway out the door.

"You ought to eat first."

"No, thanks." And he was gone.

It took all of Mary's willpower to keep from running after him, but she stood her ground. Convinced she was right, she wasn't going to give in. How *could* he expect her to pack up and move to one of those places. Just thinking about it made her shudder.

"Mama?"

Looking up, Mary saw Emily standing in the doorway, a worried look on her face. "Yes, honey?"

"Where did Daddy go?"

"He . . . er, had to go see Jimmy. Business."

"Gee, he just got home." Emily eyed her mother skeptically. "You had a fight, didn't you?"

"A disagreement, Emily. There's a difference."

But even as she said it, Mary thought, *It sure feels like a fight to me.*

JIMMY AND EVE lived in a remodeled ranch house some five miles outside the city limits. They could have afforded a mansion like Hank's, but Eve liked the country. There they kept horses, a couple of Irish setters and two stray cats, and there the kids could run as free as the wind. Eve thought she had found paradise.

As Hank drove through a gate and up a dirt road toward the house, the dogs appeared and ran alongside the car, jumping and barking. The noise brought Eve out onto the porch. When she saw the car, she waved.

Hank parked and got out. "Hello, Eve."

"Well, look who's finally come home. Just get in?"

"About an hour ago. Jimmy here?"

"Sure. Come on in. Want a drink?"

"Thanks, I'd love one."

Jimmy met them in the foyer, and Eve excused herself to go fix the drink. "How was the trip?" Jimmy asked.

"Not good. The crash hit some of our investors pretty bad."

Jimmy pursed his lips. "Let's go sit and talk about it."

The big living room-dining room was full of a mishmash of furniture that Eve had brought from her previous home. Evidence that children resided in the house was everywhere. It was homey and inviting, like the rest of the place. Certainly it didn't look like a rich man's abode. It often amazed Hank how little Jimmy was interested in the trappings of wealth. His only extravagance, if it could be called that, was his expensive clothes.

Once Eve had brought his drink and returned to the kitchen, Hank told Jimmy about East Texas and the leases he had bought there. The light came back to his eyes. "The mad scramble's on, Jimmy. I didn't have time to discuss it with you, but the leases are solid. I'd bet anything on that. I got the old gut feeling I had about Winston County." He took a swallow of his drink and waited for his partner's reaction.

He was, to put it mildly, disappointed. Jimmy raked a finger over his mouth and smiled slightly. "Yeah, the stories are beginning to be heard all the way out here. Indications are it might be bigger'n the Permian Basin. But I'm afraid this is one boom I'm going to have to miss."

Hank couldn't believe it. "Miss? But...why?"

"A lot of reasons. Eve and the kids mostly. We have a nice life here, and they wouldn't want to go to a boomtown. Eve hated Rimrock when the boom first started.''

"But, Jimmy... Those leases are first-class. I...I just wouldn't know how to operate without you."

"Sure you will. But what about the company, everything we have here?"

"Well, damn, it never occurred to me you wouldn't jump at East Texas. There's something else I want to tell you. We've been offered two-and-a-half million for Travis-Blue."

Jimmy digested that. "Who offered it?"

"National American."

"A good outfit. I figure one and a quarter million would keep me in pretty fine style for the rest of my life. What does the deal cover?"

"Our reserves in the ground and two thousand acres of leases," Hank said.

"Then I say sell."

"Just like that? No pangs of regret about selling the company we built from the ground up?"

Jimmy shook his head. "I'm not going to leave Rimrock, Hank. I know that. Eve feels that it's home, and the kids were born and raised here. Her folks are here. This town is going to be married to the oil business for decades, so I can make a pretty good piece of change as a geological consultant. The game, the chase never took hold of me the way it did you, and God knows I've already got more money than I'll ever be able to spend."

Dumbfounded, Hank shook his head. "Well, I'll be damned if all my partners aren't deserting me." He took another swallow of his drink and stared into space. "I can't pass up East Texas. Folks are gonna be talkin' about it for years. It might be the last one before the government steps in and spoils everything."

"And how does Mary feel about that?"

Hank paused to light a cigarette, which told Jimmy exactly how Mary felt about East Texas. "She says she's not going."

"So, what are you going to do?"

"I'm not sure yet. Haven't had time enough to think about it. She kinda knocked me for a loop, just sayin' no like she did."

"Women get attached to things like people and places," Jimmy offered lamely.

"Mary never did before."

"Are you sure?"

Hank was getting impatient with this conversation. To his mind, Jimmy was deserting him just as Mary was. "A woman's supposed to go where her husband does. It's as simple as that."

Jimmy said nothing, so Hank got to his feet. "I gotta be goin'. Somebody from National American's gonna be at the office some time this week. Take care of it, will you?"

Jimmy frowned. "And where will you be?"

"I've got some leases to develop, remember? Tell Eve thanks for the drink. I'll let myself out."

Hank was in a stinking, foul mood, and the one thing he didn't feel like doing was going home. He got into his car and headed back into town. Rimrock had changed a lot since he'd first seen it, shedding most of its boomtown image along the way. It had grown to a city of twelve thousand, with more arriving every week. The gin mills had pretty much been relegated to a two-block strip out on the highway to El Paso, a spot easily ignored by the community's solid citizens.

He began driving nowhere in particular. The one thought that assailed him over and over was the wish he could be content in a town like this, but it was a useless wish. As long as there was a new oil field opening up somewhere on the face of the earth, he knew he would want to be there. It was something like a sickness, like fellows got who couldn't leave liquor alone. He wondered if Mary understood that.

His life was changing more than he wanted it to. Mary didn't want to go to East Texas, so something would have to be worked out there eventually, and Jimmy wasn't going, either. It just didn't seem possible that Jimmy wasn't going to be part of his life anymore.

He drove and drove, west out of town to watch the well-lit derricks standing tall on the flat prairie and to smell the raw gas being burned off. There were so many of the gas flares that the entire oil field looked as if it were on fire. *Someday somebody's gonna find a use for that junk,* he thought. *Then a bunch more folks are gonna get rich.*

He wasn't going to miss Rimrock, and being rich no longer excited him. Once he'd gotten a real kick out of flaunting his wealth in front of the Surratts, but that was a thing of the past. Now he felt sorry for Billie Jean. She had married a wealthy drunk who now bored her, so she spent her days in an endless quest for excitement. Several times since that long-ago evening in her living room, she had made it clear that she would welcome Hank Travis's attentions. In fact, he could go over to the Holts' house this minute, doubtless find Garmon in his cups and Billie Jean ready for anything. But he wouldn't touch that with a ten-foot pole. She was desperate and kind of pathetic.

He didn't know how long he drove, but after a while, he turned back toward town. He didn't want to go home. Maybe he was afraid Mary would look at him with those big eyes and his steely resolve would crumble like clay. Damn it, he wasn't going to let her stubborn determination make him miss this newest adventure, maybe the greatest one of all. She had stepped way out of line this time.

So he drove to the Pendleton Hotel and got a room. Once inside it, he called the bootlegger he did business with. Fifteen minutes later a package was delivered to his door. A very surprised and delighted delivery boy received a five-dollar tip.

Hank set the package down on the dresser and opened the bottle inside. For the first time since his cowboying days at the YH, he deliberately planned to get drunk.

MARY GLANCED at the clock in the study for the dozenth time. In the background the radio was playing, and though the marvelous new invention had all but supplanted movies as her favorite form of entertainment, she hadn't paid any attention to the program that was on. Tonight the noise was more for company than anything. She had also tried reading, but that hadn't worked, either. Her stomach was a knot of worry. She was going to *kill* Hank Travis for putting her through this.

Finally she could stand it no longer. It wasn't too late, not even ten. Pushing herself off the sofa, she crossed the study to the phone on the desk.

"Number, please," the operator said.

"Eight-seven-three."

"Thank you."

The phone rang three times before Eve answered it. "Hello."

"Eve, Mary. I didn't wake you, did I?"

"No, we won't go to bed for half an hour yet."

"Is Hank there by any chance?"

There was a slight pause before Eve said, "No. He was earlier, but he's been gone...oh, a couple of hours, I guess. Mary, is something wrong?"

"No, I... He probably stopped by the office. Thanks, Eve. See you tomorrow."

Mary hung up, then immediately lifted the receiver again and asked the operator for the office number. The phone rang and rang before the operator came on the line. "There's no answer, ma'am. Do you want me to keep trying?"

"No, thanks. I'll try tomorrow." This time she slammed down the receiver. So that was it, she fumed. He was pouting over not getting his way, off licking his wounds or drowning his sorrows in one of those joints out on the highway. How childish!

Mary was furious. Moreover, she was stunned. She had never seen Hank behave like this. But then, she conceded, she'd never said no to him before.

Well, she was sticking to her guns, not giving an inch, because to her mind, she was one-hundred-percent right. It pained her to think Hank had so little concern for her welfare, Emily's too, that he would even consider dragging them off to one of those god-awful boomtowns.

Being mad, she discovered, helped ease the worry some. *She* had done nothing wrong, and he surely would come to see that. She accepted that he might not come home tonight at all, though where he could possibly stay she had no idea. But he was a big boy and could take care of himself. Damned if she was going to call all over town looking for him, even if she'd known where to start. Tomorrow he would probably come home with his tail between his legs, sorry as all get-out. She would accept his apologies gracefully. Then they would discuss their differences like two reasonable adults.

Turning off all the downstairs lights and locking the front door, she went up to their bedroom and dressed for bed. It took some time, but she did finally fall asleep, satisfied with the knowledge that she wasn't the one acting like a spoiled brat.

CHAPTER TWELVE

THE FOLLOWING MORNING, long after Emily had left for school and Mary was dressed for the day, Hank showed up. He came in the front door just as she was preparing to go to the office. Mary took one look at him and knew he was suffering from a terrible hangover. He looked it—unshaved and rumpled—and he certainly smelled it.

"Where have you been?" she asked, congratulating herself on her steady voice.

"I spent the night in the hotel."

"The Pendleton?"

"You know of another hotel in town?" He walked past her and up the stairs.

Mary stood at the foot, her chest heaving. Then, when she had regained her composure sufficiently, she went into the kitchen, poured a cup of coffee and carried it up to the bedroom. "You look as though you could use this," she said, handing the cup to him.

He looked at it, then snorted. "There's more to being a good wife than serving coffee," he snapped.

Mary's eyes narrowed. "What's that supposed to mean?"

"I think it should be clear. I'm gonna bathe now, and then I'm gonna pack."

"Pack?" Mary's voice cracked, and her protective shell cracked a bit. "Where are you going?"

"I have some leases to develop, and it looks like I'm gonna have to do it alone. I'll be in touch." Without taking so much as a sip of the coffee, he made for the bathroom and slammed the door behind him.

I'll be in touch. Somehow that one sentence infuriated Mary as nothing else about the whole affair had. Not, this is where I'll be, this is how you can reach me, just I'll be in touch. If he hadn't said that, she thought she might have stayed and tried to talk to him. As it was, she turned on her heel, headed downstairs, sailed out the door and drove to the office.

When she got home that afternoon, she immediately checked Hank's closet. All of his old khakis were gone, as were most of his underwear and socks. Her first thought was to wonder how on earth he would manage to get laundry done.

Then she cried.

WEEKS PASSED, and Mary received only two very unsatisfying notes from Hank. He was very busy, he said, and out in the boondocks most of the time, away from phones. Kilgore was a boom unlike any other, etc., etc. He hoped she and Emily were fine, and if they needed anything, they were to turn to Jimmy.

The days were awful. Emily, of course, knew something was wrong and tried hard to be a model of decorum, harder than a fifteen-year-old should have to, Mary thought. Jimmy and Eve, too, walked on eggshells around her. She welcomed the nights and the peace of her own home, away from curious eyes.

The first two weeks Hank was gone, Mary stayed busy. Along with Jimmy and Eve, she oversaw the dismantling of Travis-Blue Production and Exploration. Once that was an accomplished fact, she found herself much as she'd been in the early days in Rimrock—with nothing to do.

Her emotions were a confused turmoil. On one hand she would console herself with the knowledge that Hank was doing what he loved to do, perhaps what he was born to do. And he had hardly left them destitute. She lived in a mansion with servants who saw to her every wish. She had the use of two automobiles and more money than anybody needed. Jimmy and Eve were absolute rocks of support. And she had Emily—bright, perky and cheerful, too caught up in her fifteen-year-old world to suffer much because her parents had had a silly disagreement. All those positive facts made

Mary wonder why she considered Hank's absence from home such a calamity.

But then she would turn around and resentment would flare. It was unconscionable of Hank to treat them this way. My Lord, what if she or Emily got really sick? By the time someone could reach him and he got to Rimrock, one or the other could be dead.

But never once did she seriously consider packing up and following him to Kilgore. She told herself she owed Emily that much. The girl was entitled to at least one sensible parent. Mary didn't have to actually be in Kilgore to know exactly what the town was like.

HANK THOUGHT if he lived to be a hundred, he'd never again see anything to equal Kilgore as 1930 entered its final month. The town was a literal forest of derricks, and boomtown madness was all around. The streets were almost as dangerous as Chicago during Al Capone's heyday. Hank had begun carrying small wads of money that would appease holdup men without costing him very much.

As usual, it seemed that half the able-bodied men in America had found their way to East Texas, so Hank didn't have any trouble putting together a crew. Drilling on two of his leases had begun, and he was putting in sixteen-hour days, just as though those wells were all that was standing between him and the poor farm.

He had taken a room in a boardinghouse, sharing it with an old-timer named Elmer Scruggins. Elmer followed the booms, but not as a roustabout, driller or even a gambler or similar hanger-on. He covered the insanity for a newspaper back East. He was a reporter.

Hank liked Elmer because he was interesting and had a lot of adventurous yarns to tell. He liked talking to the reporter and listening to him.

And because he was beginning to feel guilt and remorse about Mary, he found himself telling Elmer a lot about his marriage and about Mary's adamant refusal to come to East Texas with him.

Elmer listened with rapt interest. Then he had a story of his own. "You know, Hank, I was just a babe in arms when Oklahoma was opened for settlement. My daddy sold our Ohio farm, packed up Mama and us kids and lit out for the Promised Land. I grew up listening to stories about what he called The Run. Oh, Lord, he could make it sound so exciting, you could almost hear the cavalry's bugle and the beating of thousands of horses' hooves across the prairie. I'd sit there as a lad and just sop it up.

"Then one evening when I was . . . oh, about sixteen, I guess, we were sitting around the kitchen table after supper, and he started in on it again.

They were stories I'd heard time and time again, but I never seemed to get tired of them. After a bit, he got up to go check on the livestock, and it was just me and Mama in the kitchen. Once he was out of hearing range, she turned to me and said, 'It wasn't so wonderful.' That was all she said, but it sure got me thinking. For Daddy it had been an adventure, something to talk about the rest of his life. For Mama it had meant leaving behind everything that was dear and familiar and heading out to live in a sod shanty for two years while they built a house and got crops in the ground. With three kids to take care of! It's different for women. Sometimes what us men think of as adventure just purely drives them crazy.''

As tired as he was, Hank couldn't sleep that night. He kept thinking of Elmer's anecdote and how it might have a lot to do with himself and Mary. Looking back, he only thought of places like Prairie Gap, Desdemona and Ranger as grand adventures, but for all he knew, Mary might simply say, "They weren't so wonderful."

The next morning he drove out to his leases, put his best man in charge, with a promise to return before Christmas, and then boarded the T & P for Rimrock.

HANK HAD NOT TOLD anyone of his arrival, and it was almost ten o'clock when the cab pulled to a halt in front of his house. A light shone from the master bedroom window and another through the frosted glass panes on either side of the front door. He quietly let himself in and climbed the stairs.

The door to the bedroom was open, and Mary was propped in bed, reading. She was dressed for sleep. Her gown had ruffles at the neckline and wrists. The dark hair she religiously brushed every night splayed around her shoulders; a ribbon held it away from her face. Hank recalled the first time he saw her, standing on the back veranda of the house at YH Ranch. In his eyes, she didn't look much older than she had then, and she was still the prettiest thing he had ever seen and the only woman he had ever truly loved.

She apparently became aware of some movement at the threshold because she looked up from her book. Her eyes widened. She gasped. "Hank!"

He closed the door, dropped his suitcase and loped across the room. Rising on her knees, Mary held out her arms, and he rushed into them, hugging her ferociously. When they parted, he kissed her several times before noticing the tears in her eyes.

"I've missed you," he said simply.

"And I've missed you."

"I'm sorry... well, for all this. I shouldn't have left the way I did."

"It's all right," she said, though it hadn't been much of the time. "You're back."

"I behaved like an ass."

"Yes, you did."

"Do you forgive me?"

Mary sniffed. "Of course I do. I've been so worried about you."

"And gettin' kinda tired of sleepin' in this big ol' bed alone, I hope."

She smiled through her tears. "Definitely."

"Then I'll take care of that." Hank sat on the edge of the bed and took off his shoes and socks. He all but ripped off his clothes and slid under the covers with her. As he pulled her soft, pliant body to his, as she fit against him as only she could, Hank thought how wonderfully right it was to be with her. For one glorious night, his restlessness was put aside, and he lost himself in the wonder that was Mary.

SEVERAL HOURS LATER, sated and content, Hank woke to find moonlight bathing the room, and Mary was looking at him. "Haven't you slept?"

She shook her head. "Not much. Little catnaps. I suppose you aren't here for long."

"I told the man I put in charge that I'd be back before Christmas, just to check up on things."

She sighed.

Hank propped himself up on an elbow and spoke earnestly. "I'm in the middle of drilling two wells. I can't just walk away from 'em. But I've gotta know what *you* want to do, Mary. I can't leave you and Emily here in Rimrock. Kilgore's over four hundred miles away from here."

"You won't be in East Texas the rest of your life. You won't be *anywhere* the rest of your life. So that's what you've chosen, and I guess I'll have to accept it. But as for me... All I want is something permanent, Hank. Emily has two more years of high school, and I want her to have a home she can always come back to and know I'll be there." Mary's eyes swept the shadowed room. "Somehow I never felt I would stay in this house the rest of my life."

Hank reached over to brush at her hair. "How about the YH?"

She shook her head. "That's Duncan's house. It would never be mine."

"Then what about the farm?"

At first Mary thought he was talking about her mother's farm, but Hank would know she wouldn't consider that in a million years. She frowned. "You mean... your family's farm?"

Hank nodded. In 1926, he had received word that both his parents were gravely ill with scarlet fever. He and Mary had hurried to South Texas, only to learn they had died within hours of each other. His father's will had stipulated that the farm be divided among the children, but only Hank's oldest brother, Norman, had wanted anything to do with it. So Hank and his siblings had eagerly relinquished their shares in the family homestead. But now...

"I thought the farm belonged to your brother now," Mary said.

"I know, but times being what they are for farmers and ranchers, I'll bet I could buy a couple of acres from Norman. He could probably use the money. I'll build you a house, any kind of house you want, and it'll be home from now on. You'd be within easy traveling distance of your mama, and I'd come home every chance I got. You remember how nice and peaceful it is there, how pretty the Frio River is. You seemed to like Norman's wife— Judy, isn't it?—real well. It'd be easy for Emily to go to college in San Antonio or even the university in Austin, if that's what she wants to do when the time comes." He searched her face intently but could read nothing there. "Well, what do you say?"

"I'm...I'm not sure, Hank. I need some time to think about it."

"Sure, honey, sure." He lifted a hand and stroked her face. "I just want you to have what you want. I want you to be happy."

She covered his hand with hers. "I know."

"I'd give anything if I could forget all about East Texas, but . . . I can't."

Mary smiled wanly. "I know that, too."

IT DIDN'T TAKE Mary long to make up her mind. Buying a few acres from Norman made sense, and it was such a peaceful place and not all that far from Crystal Creek. After all these years, it would be nice to have her family close by.

So it was decided. Hank went back to East Texas in time to see his two wells come in, but he returned before Christmas Day. Once the holiday was over, Mary put the grand mansion up for sale. With all the money pouring into Rimrock, it sold in no time, and she began to pack.

For Hank, the hardest part of it all was saying goodbye to Jimmy. He had been saying goodbye to co-workers his entire adult life, but Jimmy was different. Since that night in Gracie's all those years ago, they had been together.

"Can't imagine how you're going to get along without me, Jimmy."

"Neither can I, Hank, and that's the truth."

The two men were uneasy with each other for the first time in their long friendship. Finally, swallowing hard, Hank stuck out his hand. "So long, partner. See you in the next boom."

Jimmy took the hand and simply held it a minute. "Probably not, partner. Probably not."

Hank turned and left hurriedly before he made a complete fool of himself.

AND SO, at the beginning of 1931, Hank, Mary and Emily left Rimrock for South Texas, where they lived with Norman and Judy until their house was built. Mary had insisted it be constructed of stone— the most permanent material she could think of.

Hank was impatient, though he fought it. Those leases near Kilgore were begging to be developed, but he owed Mary a lot. The few months it took to build the house were the least he could give her.

And how she loved that house, far more than she had ever cared for the mansion in Rimrock. No detail escaped her touch. It wasn't a large house by any means—three bedrooms with two baths, still considered the ultimate in luxury, and a kitchen big enough to have a round oak table and four chairs. After years of being waited on by servants in a formal dining room, she enjoyed being in charge of her own kitchen again. She planted a garden, and Emily enrolled in high school in the nearby town of Pearsall. A bright, eager student, she fit in right away. Both Mary and Emily learned to speak and read Spanish. It was almost a necessity in the brush country south of San Antonio, where everyone was fearlessly fluent in both languages.

Twice a year, Mary and Emily drove to Crystal Creek and spent a week or so on the farm. Duncan often joined them. It was Mary's way of giving her daughter a sense of family. They also became close to Norman and Judy, so Emily became familiar with her father's relatives as well. Very deliberately, Mary set about creating the kind of life she thought Emily should have.

Except she had to do it without a husband most of the time. But Mary had become a pragmatist, and she consoled herself with the knowledge that she was only one of legions of "rig widows" in Texas. She doubted she would have seen much more of Hank had she moved to Kilgore, which, from all reports, was the kind of hellhole Ranger had been in 1917. She missed Hank, more some days than others, but she wasn't sorry to have missed East Texas.

HANK REALLY HAD, at last, found the granddaddy of them all—a huge oil field that stretched forty-five miles from north to south and up to fifteen miles from east to west. The papers began calling it the Black Giant. In Kilgore one could walk from one end of the town to the other, stepping from derrick floor to derrick floor, never once touching the ground. It was wilder than Ranger and far wilder than Rimrock had ever been. The liquor trade was brisk, but every once in a while someone would complain to the Texas Rangers. Then the town would go from wringing wet to bone dry for a few days, but that was one of the things that kept the boom interesting. While the rest of the country suffered through bread lines and soup kitchens, fortunes were being made hourly in East Texas.

Hank loved it. Had he missed it, he would have regretted it the rest of his life. He worked constantly, for his leases had proved to be unbelievably productive. He slept in doghouses, in tents, in his truck, but rarely in a bed. Some days he didn't sleep at all and ate only when it occurred to him to do so. He spent very little money on himself, though untold thousands were poured back into production, and he paid a hefty payroll.

And he lost some, too. That was part of the game. The money that was left was dutifully sent to Mary, who began a trust fund for Emily. That pleased Hank. His daughter might not see much of her father anymore, but she would, he hoped, know he was taking care of her.

Sometimes, not often but occasionally, Hank felt guilty about being such an unconventional husband and father. In the wild, early days of the East Texas boom, he made a conscientious effort to get down to South Texas once a month, but after a few days of good food, plenty of rest, visits with his beautiful daughter and his warm, loving wife, his feet would start itching again. Mary never tried to detain him, doubtless feeling it would be useless, and after a few years, their rather unorthodox marriage came to seem almost normal.

CHAPTER THIRTEEN

"YOU'RE A VERY GOOD daughter," Mary said as she watched Emily move from sink to stove. "I honestly don't know what I would do without you. But I'm fully capable of getting supper on the table myself."

"You need your rest," Emily said over her shoulder. "You haven't been out of bed all that long."

"I'm fine."

"Mama, I wish you'd let me try to find Daddy. He needs to know how sick you've been."

"Why?"

"He just does!"

"I wouldn't have the first idea where to look for him. The last letter I had from Duncan mentioned Hank's having stopped and spent a night at the YH. Said he was getting bored with Kilgore and was going back to West Texas for a while. He could be anywhere."

Emily closed a drawer with more force than necessary. "Seems to me he just goes around doing exactly what he wants to do without much thought to what might be happening here. He's always off somewhere, chasing after goodness-knows-what. Maybe he shows up at Christmas, and we're supposed to be thrilled to see him. I don't know how a man who cares about his family can do that."

"I won't stand for that kind of talk, Emily," Mary said quietly. "Your father takes care of us handsomely."

"He gives us money, I'll grant you that, but he doesn't give us anything of himself." Emily sighed. "You always defend him."

"I understand him. We've been through a lot together. I can't imagine being married to anyone else. Hank will be home soon. I can feel it." Mary smiled at her daughter, anxious to change the subject. It distressed her horribly that Emily, who once had adored Hank unreservedly, was now so openly critical of him. But she had to realize that her daughter had grown up and now looked at her father through a woman's eyes. "Something smells awfully good."

"Pot roast. I suppose I fix it too often, but it's one thing I know I can do well."

"I love it. And I especially like the hash and biscuits the next day. You're turning into a fine cook, my dear. Someday some lucky young man is going to be delighted to discover what a good cook he married. Which reminds me—how's Cal?"

A faint blush pinkened Emily's cheeks. "He's fine, just fine. He says the ranch isn't going to show much profit this year, the price of beef being what it is, but he also says that people who live close to the earth don't need a lot in the way of money."

"I suppose that's true. I think about the farm in Crystal Creek. Mama and the boys seem pretty self-sufficient."

"I think Cal must be the most contented person I've ever known."

"That really doesn't tell me what I want to know. You like him a lot, right?"

"Yes, I guess I do," Emily said, turning to lift the lid of the Dutch oven. Then she returned to the sink, where she idly glanced out the window. A car had just turned off the main road and up the gravel path that led to the house. Emily watched it a few seconds, then turned to her mother with a startled expression. "I declare, Mama, I do believe you're like one of those fortune-tellers at the carnival every year."

Mary looked up. "How's that?"

"It's Daddy! He's driving up the road right now."

Mary was on her feet in an instant and out the back door. She felt better than she had in weeks.

Hank stopped the car at the side of the house and got out, just as Mary threw herself into his arms. "Oh, I've known for days you were coming!" she cried, burying her face in his shoulder. "I just didn't know when."

As she lifted her face to receive his kiss, Mary tried not to dwell on how much of the past decade she had spent simply waiting for Hank.

"THAT SURE WAS a fine supper," Hank said, lighting a cigarette and sitting on the porch swing beside Mary. One arm slid around her shoulders to pull her close. "Emily's turning into as good a cook as you are, honey."

"She likes to cook, and that's half the battle. What brings you home this time?"

"I was worried about you. Kept havin' the feelin' something was wrong." Hank studied her intently. "You've lost some weight."

"A little."

"And your color's kinda pale. Have you been sick?"

Mary considered denying it, then thought better of it. She nodded.

"What was wrong?"

"Pneumonia."

Hank's eyes widened in horror. "Pneumonia?" he cried.

"I was over it in no time. It's not as bad as it used to be, Hank, not now that they have those new sulfa drugs. The doctor said if he'd had them back in '26, your mama and daddy wouldn't have died from scarlet fever."

"Why didn't you tell me?" He was genuinely shaken.

Mary shrugged, trying to make light of the matter. "I wasn't sure where you were, and what could you have done if you'd known? Norman and Judy were wonderful, and I was never in any real danger."

It actually hadn't been that easy. She had been very sick for a few days... sick and a little scared. She might actually have sent for him... if she'd known where he was.

"Is that the reason for the rather frosty reception I got from Emily this time?"

"Don't let her get to you, Hank. She's young and very idealistic. She wants the world to be a Busby Berkeley musical. And, too, I think she's in love."

"In love? She's too young to be in love."

Mary smiled. "She's two years older than I was when I married you."

"That's different. Times were different."

"Not all that different," Mary insisted. "The real difference is that now we're talking about *your* daughter, not someone else's."

"Who's the fellow?"

"His name is Cal McKinney. Emily met him last time we were at Mama's. He lives nearby. She was very taken with him from the beginning, and I know he's been to college to see her a couple of times."

"I hope to hell that school sees to it that the coeds are chaperoned."

Mary laughed. "Oh, Hank, how quaint! Chaperons have gone the way of the bustle."

Hank did not look pleased. "What does this McKinney fellow do for a living?"

"He's a rancher."

"Oh, great! There's a good way to starve to death."

"Cal seems very knowledgeable and industrious. Even in these terrible times, the Double C looks stable, even a little prosperous. He's a nice young man, anything but a here-today-gone-tomorrow type."

Mary bit her lip. The minute the words left her mouth she regretted them.

Hank scowled and flipped his cigarette onto the grass. "Like me?"

"Hank Travis, how dare you ask such a thing! I never thought of you that way, and you know it...or should. I'm just saying that Emily...well, the life she's led...maybe a man tied to one spot of earth appeals to her. It would have bored me to death. Anyway...I'm not sure we should get our hearts set on having a college graduate in the family. I think she and Cal want to get married...pretty soon."

"Goddammit, she can't get married! I won't allow it. What in hell does she know about being married?"

Mary smiled knowingly. "Probably fourteen times more than I did. Remember Duncan's reaction when we told him we wanted to get married?"

"That's different."

"No, it isn't," Mary said with a little laugh. "It isn't different at all. She's a woman now, and if she decides she's going to marry Cal McKinney, there's not one thing you or I can do about it."

Hank sat in silence a minute, then said, "I was in Rimrock a while back. Saw Jimmy and Eve."

Mary brightened. "How are they? Except for Christmas cards, we're almost never in touch."

"They're fine. I made them promise to make their way down here soon. Then the four of us can have a real reunion."

"That sounds like fun. Any other news from Rimrock?" she asked without much interest. She had been gone almost five years and experienced no nostalgia for the town, only occasionally for Jimmy and Eve. In fact, places like Prairie Gap and Ranger and Rimrock sometimes seemed to have happened in another lifetime. She supposed she had slipped into blissful contentment living here in the brush country, where nothing much seemed to happen, which suited her fine.

"Garmon Holt drank himself to death," Hank said.

"How awful! What about Billie Jean?"

"Hear she moved to Fort Worth to be near her in-laws." Hank snorted derisively. "She always had a fondness for the Holt name and money."

"Be kind, Hank." Mary quickly changed the subject. "So how's business?"

"Rotten ever since the goddamn government got into it. Tellin' *me* how much oil I can pump a month! Mary, everytime the government gets into something, you can bet it's gonna screw it up. I'm tellin' you—the country's going to hell in a hand basket."

"You sound like Duncan again. As I recall, the country was going to hell in a hand basket in 1912. Seems to me it's still here. In bad shape economically, I guess, but so's the whole world. You get around, Hank. Are times really as bad as we hear?"

"Pretty bad."

"But the things Mr. Roosevelt is doing are supposed to get us out of this Depression, aren't they?"

Hank scoffed. "It's gonna take a hell of a lot more than Mr. Roosevelt to get us out of this mess. Come on, let's not talk politics. It bores me."

"Emily's taking a course in political science. She says we're all going to have to get interested in it,"

Mary persisted, "because there are things going on in Europe that are frightening."

"Thank God for the Atlantic Ocean."

Mary pursed her lips. "I don't know, Hank. If we have airplanes that can fly from coast to coast now, and now Lindbergh's flown across the ocean, the Atlantic isn't a barrier anymore."

"Lord, Mary, is that all you have to worry about?" He slipped his arm around her shoulders and gave her a squeeze. "I've been thinking about staying a spell this time, honey. Do you think you could get used to having a full-time husband for a while?"

Mary's eyes widened. "Are you serious?"

"Completely."

"You'll be bored to death in a week."

"No, I promise. I really want to stay."

"Oh, Hank...that's the best medicine I could ever have!"

Seeing her bright eyes and happy smile, he pulled her close. "Why did you stay with me all these years, Mary? It can't have been easy."

"That's a silly question. I love you."

"But other than that. You can love a person and get so damned disgusted you want to run."

"Well, I never did," she said decisively. "Even if there were times when things...well, weren't exactly what I wanted them to be, I never once thought of leaving. I always knew I couldn't be happy without you."

A powerful feeling came over Hank. He wasn't sure how to describe it. He'd never put much stock in fate or destiny or whatever one wished to call it, but his thoughts strayed back to the day an eighteen-year-old kid trudged along a lonely country road. If anyone other than Duncan MacGregor had stopped to offer the boy a ride, the best things in his life might not have happened.

"You know, honey, I've made many a good deal in my day, but damned if you weren't the best. To my dying day I'll think asking you to marry me was the smartest thing I ever did."

"You didn't ask me," Mary reminded him. "I asked you."

Hank chuckled. "You did, didn't you? Then the smartest thing I ever did was say yes. And I'm still surprised and grateful you stuck it out."

"You know how I dreamed of adventure. If I hadn't stayed with you, how in the world could I ever have seen exotic places like Prairie Gap, Ranger, Rimrock...."

A flood of memories washed over Hank. "God, it was fun!" he exclaimed, then immediately sobered. "And it'll never be the same again. Like being a kid. Once it's gone, it's gone forever. And the sad thing is—it disappeared while I was standin' there watchin'."

"I think you're getting maudlin on me. Something will come along to take its place. The night air's getting chilly. Let's go inside, and I'll fix coffee." Mary kissed him sweetly, then stood and took him by the hand. "We have the rest of our lives to plan."

Hand in hand they ambled into the house and began talking about tomorrow and all the tomorrows left to them.

EPILOGUE

J.T. PUT DOWN his pen, stared out the window a minute, then returned to his task.

In many ways the following year was the best one of Hank and Mary's marriage. Much to her surprise, he did not return to the oil patch, though he read the papers and complained loudly about how the government was ruining the business. Mainly, however, the two of them slipped into quiet and contented domesticity. It was wonderful that they had that year.

In 1936, they presided over Emily's marriage to Calvin McKinney, and when I was conceived, Mary impatiently awaited the birth of her first grandchild, anticipating the new role with great pleasure.

But she never saw me. In 1937, only a few months before I was born, she again contracted pneumonia, and all the drugs in the world couldn't help her. She was just too sick.

With Mary gone and Emily married, Hank again took up the life of a nomad, working the rigs, never staying anywhere for long. As the years rolled by, he grew crustier, harder and more foulmouthed, but there always was a gallantry about him that's seldom seen today. Throughout my childhood, he was an almost mythical figure to me. He'd show up without warning and entertain me with his oil patch yarns. Then he'd be off again, sometimes disappearing in the middle of the night. To avoid saying goodbye, I've often thought. My mother was always delighted to see him arrive... and just as delighted to see him go.

Whatever else he was, he was a character, the last of an independent breed the world will never see again.

"J.T., surely you've finished that thing by now. It seems you've been working on it forever."

J.T. looked up to see his wife, Cynthia, standing at the threshold, their daughter, Jennifer, propped on her hip. He put down his pen, rubbed his eyes and made a neat stack of the papers he had written. "Yes, I'm done," he said. "There's nothing left to say."

"Then come on. Lettie Mae says supper will be on the table in five minutes flat."

J.T. pushed back his chair with the heel of a boot, then reached in a drawer, brought out a manila envelope and placed the papers inside. Now it really was time to say goodbye. During the project, Hank had seemed as alive and well as he'd been many, many years ago, but now it was time to put him to rest.

"So long, Grandpa," he said. "See you in the next boom."